D1103802

Broke Down Engine

Broke Down Engine
and Other Troubles with Machines

RON GOULART

Collier Books
New York, New York
Collier-Macmillan Ltd., London

These stories are reprinted by permission.

THE TROUBLE WITH MACHINES, copyright © 1968 by Ron Goulart, originally appeared in *Playboy*. BROKE DOWN ENGINE (under the title "Broke and Hungry, No Place to Go"), copyright 1969 by Universal Publishing and Distributing Corporation, originally appeared in *Galaxy*, November 1969. LOFTHOUSE (under the title "A Man's Home Is His Castle"), copyright © 1969 by Ron Goulart, originally appeared in *Playboy*. CALLING DR. CLOCKWORK, copyright © 1965 by Ziff-Davis Publishing Company. PRINCESS #22, copyright © 1962 by Mercury Press, Inc., originally published in *The Magazine of Fantasy and Science Fiction*. ALL FOR LOVE (under the title, "By Way of Mars"), copyright 1965 by Galaxy Publishing Corporation, originally appeared in *Worlds of Tomorrow*. THE KATY DIALOGUES, copyright © 1958 by Mercury Press, Inc., originally published in *The Magazine of Fantasy and Science Fiction*. NOBODY STARVES, copyright © 1963 by Mercury Press, Inc., originally published in *The Magazine of Fantasy and Science Fiction*. MUSCADINE, copyright © 1958 by Mercury Press, Inc., originally published in *The Magazine of Fantasy and Science Fiction*. DISPOSAL, copyright © 1969 by Mercury Press, Inc., originally published in *The Magazine of Fantasy and Science Fiction*. TO THE RESCUE, copyright © 1965 by Mercury Press, Inc., originally published in *The Magazine of Fantasy and Science Fiction*. JOKER FOR HIRE (under the title "Anything For Laughs"), copyright 1963 by Ziff-Davis Publishing Company. TERMINAL, copyright © 1965 by Ziff-Davis Publishing Company.

Copyright © 1971 by Ron Goulart

All rights reserved. No part of this book may be reproduced or transmitted in any form or by any means, electronic or mechanical, including photocopying, recording or by any information storage and retrieval system, without permission in writing from the Publisher.

The Macmillan Company
866 Third Avenue, New York, N.Y. 10022
Collier-Macmillan Canada Ltd., Toronto, Ontario

Library of Congress Catalog Card Number: 78-122292

First Collier Books Edition 1972
Broke Down Engine is also published in a
hardcover edition by The Macmillan Company.

Printed in the United States of America

Contents

Feel like a broke down engine, mama,
Ain't got no drivin' wheel.
If you ever been down and lonesome,
You know exactly how a poor man feels.

—Blind Willie McTell,
Broke Down Engine Blues

Foreword: The Way Things Don't Work

"There comes a point (this is the challenge facing modern, technological, Western man) when the cult of technique destroys feeling, undermines passion, and blots out individual identity. . . . It is not at all clear that technology and eros are compatible, or can even live without perpetual warfare. The lover, like the poet, is a menace on the assembly line."

—Rollo May,
Love and Will

This is a book about us and machines. About the remarkable machines and gadgets we're beginning to live with now and particularly about the awesome engines and mechanical devices that will greet us up ahead in the future. Computers, robots, plastic hearts, androids and all sorts of other mechanisms which are supposed to serve man. In the thirteen stories here I'm concerned not only with what the

machines can do for us but with how we will get along with
them. What sort of relations, with what consequences, we
may have. This is, therefore, sort of a guidebook on how to
live with machines, illustrated with a dozen or so case
histories from the future.

We've all heard about the advent of technological man,
of *homo mechanicus,* that future man who is going to be
involved even more intimately than we are with machines
and mechanisms. I use these stories to anticipate, to specu-
late on what sort of encounters this technological man will
have in his mechanical world. The event around which
many of the stories turn is that moment when things stop
working just right. This is the reason they're grouped under
the title *Broke Down Engine.* It seems to me that the
moment of breakdown can often also be the moment of
truth.

Ron Goulart

Broke Down Engine

1

The Trouble with Machines

The long-legged blonde on the chrome motor scooter
seemed to have a fever. As she blurred into the fog on the
coastal highway, Bill Majors drove his Volkswagen bus into
the back end of a produce truck. The little bus quivered
and buckled slightly, hopped ahead when the truck made
a stalling stop. In the shadowed storage area behind Bill,
the sky-blue refrigerator he was hauling fell over backward
and made an angry sound.

"Oh, boy," Bill said, and hit his own brakes hard.

The refrigerator got itself upright and, after a faint whir,
handed Bill a yellow note.

"Not now," said Bill. He clicked off the engine of his bus.

The vanguard of a motorcycle gang shot out of the fog
behind Bill and rear-ended the bus. The refrigerator top-
pled forward and slammed against Bill's shoulder.

"Take it easy, Maximo," said Bill.

The blue refrigerator snorted and got itself standing again. It whirred and slipped Bill another note.

Bill wouldn't read the messages. "Don't do this in front of people," he said, straight-lipped. The first two words of the top message were, "You *schmuck!*"

The produce-truck driver had a languid face. He rested his large hands on the window ledge beside Bill. "You didn't come talk to me, so I'll come and talk to you."

"This fog," said Bill.

"My cases of soybeans and kelp are all topsy-turvy," said the driver, scratching at the freckled skin below the rolled-up cuffs of his plaid shirt.

The leader of the motorcycle gang came and stood beside the truck driver. "Don't let the death's heads and red devils on our outfits fool you. I'm David G. Germershausen and that's my high school civics class back there. Our project today is to dress up like a band of roving speedway hoodlums. Afterward we'll have a picnic lunch."

"I got distracted by all this fog," said Bill. "Sorry." The refrigerator was poking him on the shoulder with a new note. "Now I'll just get out my insurance plate and we can send a report in on the nearest telephone slot."

"Your refrigerator has little arms and hands," said the produce-truck driver. "Is that new in refrigerators?"

"Yes, it is." Bill gave the refrigerator a negative hunch. "Won't be in the stores until, oh, a couple of years. Until 1976 at the earliest. This is a test model."

"Could I bring the kids over for a look?" asked Germershausen. He twisted one of the jewels in the eye of his coat's front skull. "They're very interested in gadgetry."

"No, actually," Bill told him, "this machine is sort of secret and when the front office learns about even this little incident, I'll be really criticized." He reached into the left-hand breast pocket of his driving tunic and took out an identification packet. "Yes, here are all my insurance cards. The pile-up was my fault. I'll mark the responsibility square, there. Do you have a phone in your truck? We can slot this right to the insurance company and let them make the report to the highway patrol."

"Sure," said the truck driver. "Then we can all resume our journeys." A silver trailer swung by, honking angrily. The produce-truck driver thumbed his nose, then took the insurance charge plate and cards. "I'll handle it, Mr. Netcher. Charles Netcher is your name, huh? They call you Charlie?"

"Chuck," said Bill.

"Your Volks going to run okay?" asked Germershausen as the driver returned to his truck.

Bill turned on the switch and the electric engine hummed. "Sounds fine. You're sure your pupils are all in good shape?"

"Yes." The refrigerator dropped another note over Bill's shoulder and the teacher asked, "What are the little memos for?"

"Household hints," said Bill. "Another new feature. Also confidential." The yellow note in his lap read: *You dumb nitwit! You've probably blown the whole thing. Get us the hell out of here and stop shooting the breeze!*

Germershausen adjusted the bill of his cap and nodded. "Yes, my wife would like that. What company is going to put this baby on the market?"

"That," said Bill, "I'm not at liberty to say."

"Well, can I give you my home address and have you send my wife a brochure in 1976?"

"Fine," said Bill.

The refrigerator snorted.

Fifteen miles from the gate of the Carlquist Estate, the big blue refrigerator began shuffling restlessly and exuding wispy yellow smoke. After a full minute of that, the machine shot out a hand and gave Bill a note.

"I told you I can't read when I'm driving." Bill hunched

and squinted through the thick Pacific fog. He was 100 miles down the coast from the Carmel laboratory of Dr. Jack Mackinson, and before he could complete his mission, in Southern California, he had to stop at the eclectic hilltop estate of Con Carlquist. The delay couldn't be avoided. Carlquist, who controlled Bogman/Carlquist Appliances, was funding this whole operation and had insisted on a look at Maximo. Maximo was what Dr. Mackinson called the refrigerator.

Bill dropped his glance for an instant, returned to studying the blurred road. "Hey," he said and grabbed up the latest note.

The memo said, "Don't drive so fast! I'm carsick."

"Carsick?" asked Bill. "How can you be any kind of sick? You're a machine. A robot built to look like a refrigerator."

"I have feelings," said the next note. "Don't talk to me so harshly."

"Me harsh? You've been dropping nasty remarks since we left Mackinson's damn lab."

"Everyone yearns to communicate. Don't scorn me for having a deep need to express my thoughts and emotions."

To get a machine such as Maximo—at present, anyway, though Bogman/Carlquist was working on it—you had to deal with eccentric people like Dr. Mackinson. The doctor had programed a lot of useless stuff into Maximo's brain. Including the entire contents of the Great Books. And Dr. Mackinson had built into Maximo someplace the ability to print notes, to make comments. Another useless function; but you couldn't argue with the mavericks like Dr. Mackinson.

Bill watched the far lane of the six-lane speedway for some guidepost to indicate they should turn off for Carlquist. Finally he asked the machine, "Did that crash we had hurt you, Maximo?"

"Maximo is a harsh name. A fittingly brutal name for a killer."

"Don't start having qualms already." Bill saw CARL-QUIST PRIVATE ESTATE NEXT LEFT NO ADMITTANCE in the rolling mist and swung the Volkswagen bus carefully into the leftmost lane. "The crash joggled you, didn't it? Because, look, you're a machine. A machine we want to do just one simple thing for us, Maximo."

"The trouble with machines," said Maximo's next note, "is that they don't care."

The stopping at the Carlquist Estate was slowing the whole job down and now Maximo might even need repairs. That damned muckraker Lionel Mitchum was sitting in his testing center in Santa Riorita Beach, ready to rip the lid the rest of the way off the whole appliance business. And here was Maximo, built to solve the problem. Getting them together, though, was taking much too long.

"Death and killing," printed Maximo. "The oldest profession. My soul sickens when I realize what I am being thrust into."

Bill didn't answer. The little bus began climbing the pebbled road that wound uphill to the guarded walls of Con Carlquist's estate. Eucalyptus trees and transplanted redwoods framed the tight twisting roadway. Maximo handed over two more notes and Bill ignored them. He was hoping the robot would joggle back to normal before the interview. The road was bumpy enough.

Bill stopped the bus too close to the solid-beam gates and that made the guard drop the taco he'd been eating. The green-uniformed man let the taco stay in the ferns along the high stone wall. He snatched up a burp gun from the kitchen stool beside him and approached Bill.

"Sorry," Bill said out into the tumbling fog.

"Easy," said the mustached guard. "Keep the mitts in sight, buster. No fancy stuff or I start dealing out death with my roscoe."

"I thought it was pistols they called roscoes," said Bill. "I'm Bill Majors. The entrance password is: 019/141/198/572."

The guard grinned, lowering the gun barrel. "2004/218/241. Is that the countersign?"

"240 at the end. Otherwise, okay."

"Welcome aboard, Mr. Majors. Lunch is in half an hour." He tilted his head, his misted mustache serving as a pointer. "I guess she, up atop the wall there, distracted you and caused you to almost drive into me and send me crashing through the hot hinges of the devil's domain. Am I correct?"

Sitting on the wall, with her long bare legs hanging over the edge, was the feverish blonde who had caused Bill to get distracted before and drive into the soybean truck. "How can she sit up there? Isn't there broken glass on top?"

"She's Beverly Lee Tate," the guard explained. "Mr. Carlquist's private secretary. Watch out for her, Mr. Majors, because dames can be deadly."

"You must read a lot of—"

"Hard-boiled detective stories. Right. I have my own facsimile printer in my quarters. I buy four a day. Well, you'd best drive on in."

"But how does she manage to sit up there?"

"Had me clear a place for her. Nobody argues with Beverly Lee Tate. She likes to lounge up there and watch if any young fellows drive up to the gates, though they seldom do."

"Oh," said Bill. He started the bus and rolled onto the estate grounds after the guard had worked all the combination locks and swung the high thick gates slowly open.

Con Carlquist moved his wineglass and fingered a toggle beside his plate. "This is linked out with computer center in Santa Ana," he said across the stiff white lunch table to Bill. "We used to have to time-share our computers with a lending library in Gardena. When I assumed full control of

Bogman/Carlquist, I smoothed functions out." He was tall, grinning, the wrinkles on his 60-year-old face white on his sunburned skin.

"I already know the Lionel Mitchum situation pretty well," said Bill. Carlquist's chair was in front of a glass wall showing the thick forests of the estate, the gingerbread guest chalets and the low geodesic storage warehouses. The mist spun and danced in the wind from the forest. Bill turned away from Carlquist and the view.

Beverly Lee Tate smiled at him. She had a miniaturized conference recorder sitting in the palm of one slender warm hand and she was stroking it absently, the way you stroke a pet lizard. "We don't need any more info input, Con. Forget about whatever else our computers have on file. Mr. Majors has outlined the how and why of things. I think his ideas for getting Maximo into Lionel Mitchum's private testing lab are fine. Provided we can be sure the key man on the consumer board is working for us."

"He is, certainly," said Bill. "We have his written agreement. It's even notarized."

"Wasn't that risky?" asked Carlquist.

"He had his own notary seal," explained Bill. "Mr. Carlquist, as soon as you inspect Maximo, I know you'll be more than satisfied."

"That's right, Con," said the blonde girl.

"You play tennis a lot?" Bill asked her.

"No, not at all. I just like to wear shorts."

"That Lionel Mitchum," said Carlquist, his grin expanding and contracting. "That no-good muckraking bastard. We can't afford to have that book of his, that *Infernal Machines*, come out. His magazine articles have done us enough harm. Bogman/Carlquist can't drop any further. If only the Government had cooperated more openly. We've had seven decades of these guys. Steffens, Sinclair, Packard and Nader, and still Washington won't give us a law against

muckraking. Well, nobody's going to do Bogman/Carlquist
dirt."

"We all agree, Con," said Beverly Lee. "The solution Mr.
Majors has come up with is excellent."

"Actually," said Bill, "the solution is a joint effort of
myself and my superiors in the trouble-shooting department
of the San Francisco office of Bogman/Carlquist. We all
worked on the research and the tracking down and negotiat-
ing with Dr. Mackinson."

"What's Dr. Mackinson like?" asked the blonde Beverly
Lee.

"He's short," said Bill.

"The man's made a half dozen other robots," said Carlquist, "for similar jobs, as I understand."

"Right," said Bill, "and each one has been successful.
Once we place Maximo in Lionel Mitchum's testing rooms,
we're set. To our muckraking friend, Maximo will appear
on the surface to be a regular 1974-model refrigerator, sky-
blue shade."

"The industry is calling that shade bluebell blue this
year," corrected Carlquist.

"Sorry, yes, bluebell blue. So Lionel Mitchum thinks Maximo is simply another dangerous shoddy appliance, a target
for his forthcoming exposé book."

"However," said Beverly Lee, "Maximo only seems to be
a refrigerator. He's also a highly mobile robot, with power-
ful hands and limbs. Programed to stalk, hunt and kill."

"To kill only Mitchum," said Carlquist. "Isn't that right,
Majors?"

Bill hesitated. Dr. Mackinson was vague. Bill's superiors
had hinted that Maximo had done something to one of Dr.
Mackinson's part-time cleaning women during the testing
stages. Bill hadn't favored driving over 400 miles with
Maximo, but it fit in with the carefully constructed cover
stories they'd built. "Yes, that's correct, Mr. Carlquist."

"Very good." The grin flexed. "We'll take care of Lionel

Mitchum. And Maximo is also designed, I have been led to believe, to destroy Mitchum's files and burn down the guy's whole setup. All of which will give the outside world the notion Lionel Mitchum went too far in testing some dubious appliance and got himself frizzled."

Beverly Lee rose, knifing one slender arm straight into the air and stretching so her breasts rose under the tennis jersey. "The public will realize you shouldn't mess around too much with machines, that you should simply accept them."

"Let's get out to your van now and take a good look at this Maximo," said Carlquist. "If you've had enough lunch."

"Perhaps a little more tempura?" asked Beverly Lee.

"Since you're all standing," Bill said, getting up, "we can go now."

"Excellent," said the warm girl.

The Volkswagen bus was parked beneath a thick dark tree and circled by chill mist. "You understand," Bill said as they approached, "Maximo may be surly. It's tied in with the killer instinct."

"All the better," said Carlquist.

Beside the blonde girl, Bill asked, "Aren't you cold without a coat?"

"No. My body temperature always remains an even one hundred. Cold never bothers me."

Bill opened the back of the bus. Maximo was not there. "He's run off," mumbled Bill. He reached in and picked up the yellow note resting where Maximo had stood.

"He really is mobile," said Carlquist.

Beverly Lee Tate took the note out of Bill's hand."

" 'Goodbye to all this!' What's that mean, Bill?"

"Well," said Bill.

The mustached guard raised his flash and searchlighted the thick night fog. "Did Carlquist give you a tongue-lashing?" he asked Bill.

"Not exactly." But if they didn't find Maximo soon, Bill's job with the San Francisco office of Bogman/Carlquist wouldn't be there any more.

A party of six assorted Carlquist Estate employees passed Bill's group of five. "Anything?" asked the mustached guard, whose name was Greyfriar.

"We checked storage warehouse number one and storage warehouse number two," called the associate gardener. "No sign. You?"

"Nothing yet."

A pastry chef shivered. "I don't like it. A crazy refrigerator roaming the grounds. It's spooky."

Bill shook his head. He had wanted to search for Maximo by himself. Too many people meant a chance of a leak. But Con Carlquist was mad, and anxious and willing to risk security for results. "He's really harmless," Bill told the two parties of men. "Things have been built up out of proportion."

Leaves crackled downhill and another guard came running up through the trees. "Good Lord!" he said.

"What?" asked Greyfriar.

"Good Lord, good Lord!"

"He's seen something creepy," said the pastry chef, shining his lantern on the shaking guard.

"He got Curly," said the guard.

"Curly?"

"That refrigerator got Curly," said the thin man, his head ticking. "Good Lord! The refrigerator broke into Curly's quarters and strangled him with those funny little hands. Good Lord! I saw it through the open door. There was no time to save Curly, so I escaped by way of the rumpus-room window."

"Is the machine still down there?" asked Greyfriar, his mustache pointing.

"He set fire to the chalet me and Curly and Buck live in. You can just barely see it if the fog lifts. Downhill, blazing like a bonfire. We'd better get it put out before the fire spreads."

"That refrigerator," said the pastry chef. "It's gone too far now. Let's forget about capturing it. We should smash it good, knock it down and jump up and down on it and rip out its works and scatter them."

"Now, wait," put in Bill, "Mr. Carlquist wants Maximo found, not destroyed."

"You didn't see Curly, buddy," said the thin guard.

"Let's get that damn thing," someone yelled. "Damn lousy machine."

"First we get the fire under control," said Greyfriar. "Then we can run that fridge to ground and fix it for good."

"No, now," said Bill. "It's awfully expensive, remember." He moved aside as the men began to run down through the misty forest. "Use discretion with him," he called. He'd have to find Maximo himself and talk him back into the bus.

Beyond the woods were more chalets and storage domes. The first dome Bill searched was filled with Carlquist's past hobbies. Cardboard boxes packed with foreign-stamp approval sheets, knickknack shelves thick with crystal cats, packing crates overflowing with stuffed birds and the articulated skeletons of reptiles. But no Maximo. Bill wandered through and around the dusty dome, his flashlight swinging slowly in his hand. Outside, he could hear, at a distance, the search parties fighting the chalet fire. As he left the storage dome, the wind suddenly blew the fog high above the treetops and Bill noticed an apple orchard to his left. He entered it, calling softly, "Maximo."

Fog was seeping down thick through the tree branches again. A red-and-yellow lady apple rolled across the soft ground and bonked Bill's ankle. Off on the left, a muffled whir sounded and something tapped cautiously against the bark of a tree. "Maximo, is that you?" Bill asked carefully. He moved toward the subdued humming. "Don't make too much noise, if that is you, because there are bunches of guys out there who want to dismantle you."

He bumped into something blue. Bill felt with the palm of his hand. A tiny arm caught his sleeve and gave him a yellow note. "Where am I?"

"What have you got now, amnesia? Don't you remember setting fire to Curly's chalet?"

Maximo produced another memo-sized note. "I don't remember anything after you made that dumb mistake and drove into the garbage truck."

"It was a produce truck. We haven't got time to debate the details now, though. You've been on a rampage and there are all kinds of guys running around this estate, looking for you with lanterns and torches." Bill took hold of one of Maximo's springy arms. "I don't know if I'll be able to talk them out of doing you violence, so we better try to sneak back to the main house. Carlquist should be able to keep anybody from hurting you."

"You're more worried about screwing up another job than you are about my welfare."

"No more note passing, Maximo. And try to whir as quietly as you can. Are you able to bend down some? Or at least hunker a little?"

The big blue refrigerator let itself fall forward and little running wheels appeared at its four corners. "Thanks to you, I have to crawl around a crab-apple orchard on my stomach."

Bill crumpled the note into his coat pocket. He listened, heard nothing of the search parties. "We'll head over that way, Maximo, through the trees and up by that row of chalets. This bunch of houses seems to be dark—nobody there. We can pick up the bridle paths and get the hell back to the big house. Want me to help you steer yourself?"

Maximo gave a growl and they started through the misty orchard. The robot had some trouble cornering but otherwise moved well in the horizontal position. They cleared the orchard and began climbing over thick wet grass, through tangles of dry-leaved underbrush. Bill realized the machine had halted when he stumbled over it.

A warm slender hand picked him off the turf. "Bill, come this way."

It was Beverly Lee Tate, still in tennis shorts and jersey. "I've got to get Maximo back to the main house," Bill told her.

"You won't be able to, the men are closing in." She pointed at the fog, half turning. "My chalet is just up there. Hurry, you can both hide there." She squeezed his hand, turned fully and hurried away.

"OK," agreed Bill. He nudged the refrigerator and Maximo stood upright and ran through the fog after Beverly Lee.

The long lean girl had turned on one low lamp in the rustic living room. "Bolt the door," she told Bill.

"If they look in here," Bill said after locking the door and closing the quail-print curtains, "it's going to look strange. With a big refrigerator standing in the middle of the living room."

The girl crossed to a redwood door and opened it, fingering on a faint bluish light. "Get in the kitchen, Maximo. Purloined-letter sort of logic. Nobody will notice a refrigerator in the kitchen, even an extra one. Hurry."

Maximo rolled across the Navaho rugs and into the kitchen. When the door closed on the machine, Bill could still see a strip of blue light along the floor. "It's warm in here," he said.

Beverly Lee lowered herself to a leather sofa, put her bare tan knees tight together and cupped them with her hands. "I worked out the heating system myself. It's—to simplify considerably—a sort of transistorized sauna system. I'm fond of steam."

Bill leaned as the girl raised herself. He kissed her. It was slightly unsettling, like standing too close to a sun lamp.

He was moving his hand toward her waist when he heard a great ratcheting noise from the kitchen. "Hey," he said.

Beverly Lee cupped warm hands over his ears and kissed him again. "It's only Maximo settling in."

She stretched back on the leather sofa. Putting a knee on the middle cushion, Bill started to swing his other foot up off the floor. He stopped. From under the kitchen door, a small silver balance wheel came rolling. "A cogwheel just rolled out of your kitchen, Beverly Lee."

"Ignore it," the girl said softly.

The little wheel spun across one rug and collapsed on the second. Bill crossed and picked it up. "This looks like it could be part of Maximo." He held the wheel up to the girl. "Beverly Lee, is this part of Maximo?"

The girl sat up and folded her arms under her breasts. She shrugged.

Bill grabbed the knob and yanked the kitchen door open. A wide earth-brown stove scurried across the floor and, with tiny arms, stuffed scraps of metal into its open oven. "You can't," Bill started to say.

The stove stopped, back in place against the blue-lit wall. Its oven roared for a second with an intense flame. Through the view window, Bill witnessed the last of Maximo burn away.

"Your stove," he said at the doorway.

"Yes," replied Beverly Lee. "I built it about six months ago. I've done considerable research in the field of applied heat. I like warmth, as you know."

"A robot stove that can kill," said Bill.

"It doesn't kill people. I don't agree with Dr. Mackinson's notions about that," she said. "A machine that kills violates the rules of robotics, I feel. No, I built the stove in anticipation of Maximo."

"Oh, so?"

"If he hadn't gone goofy, I'd have had both of you in here hours ago."

"But Carlquist," said Bill. He was closer to the big stove. It said HOTPOINT over its oven.

"I don't really work for Con Carlquist," said Beverly Lee. She leaned against the kitchen door jamb. "Companies like Bogman/Carlquist still don't have any use for a girl with my kind of quirky thermal notions. Nor do they have much in the way of ethics."

"Ethics? You just now murdered a pretty expensive machine."

"To keep it from going down and killing Lionel Mitchum," said the warm girl. "You seem to think that your kind of industrial espionage works only one way."

"You're—what did they call it in my business spying class—you're a double agent," Bill told her. "You're working here and for Mitchum, too."

"Of course. Lionel Mitchum didn't get where he is by being a sitting duck." She backed away. From behind the sofa she pulled a tan suitcase.

"Boy," said Bill, "how can I tell Bogman/Carlquist that a stove ate my refrigerator?"

"I have to get away now," said Beverly Lee.

"I guess I'm out of a job."

"Can I give you a ride anyplace?"

"I still have the VW bus."

"If you go back to get it, you'll have to talk to Con Carlquist."

"I suppose there are job opportunities around Santa Riorita Beach," Bill reflected. "That where you're heading?"

"Initially."

"Can we both fit on your motor scooter?"

"Sure. Come on."

Bill followed the girl out of the chalet. "I was thinking about leaving Bogman/Carlquist after the first of the year, anyway."

Beverly Lee cut around the house to where her scooter

was parked. They passed below the kitchen window and Bill noticed that the glass had been smashed out. In a rose-bush, surrounded by a sprinkling of glass, was a small yellow memo. It must have been written by Maximo just before he was dismantled. Bill reached out and pulled the note free.

"Yes," Beverly Lee said, "maybe this is the chance you needed to really start that climb."

Bill read the message. "Another fine mess, you *schmuck,*" it said. He folded it into his pocket and climbed onto the back of the motor scooter.

2

Broke Down Engine

Warren Milson frowned politely at the computer and told it to stop singing. "It's distracting," he said, looking up from the sprawl of punch cards in his lap.

The computer, Simulator RR-G8, was built into a third of the wall across from Milson. It had a pebbled black surface, some of its spools slightly askew. "Well, let's get going then," it said from its speech grid. "Almost ten o'clock."

"Calm down," Milson straightened in his work chair and used both hands to touch the cards.

"Feel like a broke down engine, mama, ain't got no drivin' wheel," sang the computer in a broad nasal voice. "Yes, I feel like a broke down engine that ain't got no drivin' wheel."

"Come on. Be quiet."

"When you're broke and hungry," replied the computer in its own voice, "it helps to sing the blues."

Milson said, "Don't keep making fun. Stop now." He studied a card, Will Fabin's. There wasn't much doubt. Fabin was ready for Questionnaire 31 and a run through the simulator. "Okay, here's one." He hesitated, put the punch card on the conveyor rack leading into the machine. "And another." Mrs. Horowitz. Finally Milson settled on twenty name cards.

"Not an even two dozen?" asked Simulator RR-G8.

"The quota is twenty an hour," said Milson. "That's what the Greater Los Angeles Nutrition Office says."

"You keep aiming for the minimum," said the computer, its speech grill rattling faintly. After whirring for a moment it added, "Okay, I got Questionnaire 31 off to all our deadbeats. Now what?"

"We wait for the replies, as usual." Milson went to his long and wide work table and fingered the correspondence toggle.

"If you had more status, more drag," said the computer, "we could have a window in this office. The Greater Los Angeles skyline, that's some sight. I'd like to see that, and Knott's Berry Farm."

"They tore Knott's Berry Farm down in 1987," said Milson. "Nobody could take a computer there anyway."

"Let the spades in anyplace, but a computer it's different."

Milson held his watch to his ear and it whispered, "The time is 10:01." As the letters and reports unreeled on the table scanner, Milson said, "I'll take my morning coffee break now."

"Go ahead, you don't need my approval."

Milson punched the coffee knob on the wall panel. From the food slot over his work table appeared a styro cup of near coffee. Milson lifted the cup out, sniffed at it. "Cold."

"You're lucky we have coffee at all. That last food riot in the Santa Monica Sector, they burned the soy bean crop."

Milson sipped the cold near coffee. He watched the scanner. "That's great. Thirty-four percent of the people in the Beverly Hills Sector don't believe there's a famine there at all."

"The computers who take those attitude things are up on floor twenty-six here. I know them. All their stuff is faked. They don't even try to question every resident, on the intrude circuit. Slipshod."

"Okay, be quiet while I catch up."

"Did you have trouble getting to work in the tube today?"

"Because of the emergencies I'm staying in the dorm up on twenty-five these nights. You know that."

"Oh, yeah," said the computer. "How come you never married, Warren?"

"I'm only twenty-seven," Milson told the machine. He brushed down his pale short hair. "I wanted a career, helping people, you know. I'm not like some guys, out for just money. All these famines. The defoliation accidents, especially those big ones in Kansas and Iowa. The food riots all over, more and more of them. I decided when I was at UC Senior Campus #22 I had to help. I can marry when the country is more settled, back on the track again."

"And you eat better working for the Greater Los Angeles Nutrition Office, too."

Milson didn't answer. The next batch of micro mail was from people protesting either food cut-off orders or removals. One letter was signed Ortega. Milson remembered old Mrs. Ortega. Her punch card had the *r* in her last name printed in reverse. Maria Lemos Ortega. No, Amelia Lemos Ortega. Something like that. Milson caught up the dictate mike and said into it, "Send forms 200A and 200B out on all the protest mail, whichever applies."

"Here we go," announced the computer. "The questionnaires are coming in. Hey, fifteen back already."

"So fast?"

"Sure, I can find anybody in Greater Los Angeles. No matter where they are. I don't depend only on the intrude circuit. I have lots of other ways. I'm hooked into every room in GLA, even this one."

"Oh, so?" said Milson. He swallowed coffee. "What's the result on the questionnaires so far?"

"They're all deadbeats to me."

"Yes, but we have a procedure to follow. First they have to get a doubtful welfare rating and then we send them Questionnaire 31. That has to come before running a full-scale Life Simulation."

"Circumlocution and red tape," said the machine. "Uh huh, uh huh, okay, uh huh. I got all twenty back now and eleven of the twenty deadbeats flunked out, meaning they have less than minimal social utility. So let's run the Life Simulation."

"Mrs. Horowitz on your list?"

"Second in line. You know her?"

"The printer reversed the *r* on her card. No, I don't actually know her."

"Give me the go-ahead order, Warren. Like protocol insists."

"Proceed to run Life Simulations on those Greater Los Angeles Nutrition Office charges who have just failed Questionnaire 31, Simulator RR-G8." Milson turned away from the computer and looked at a blank vermilion wall. Maybe he should petition for a window. He tried to see in his mind what the view from his office would show of Greater Los Angeles.

After a moment Milson returned to the work table and ran off the last of the hour's communications. The national food riot count was up and Philadelphia had burned down. Milson shook his head and toggled the scanner off.

"Hey, that was a good batch," said the computer. "Nine takeouts."

"So many?" asked Milson. He'd been reaching for a packet of welfare cards to select the next group of Greater Los Angeles Nutrition Office charges for Questionnaire 31. "Give me their names."

"No need to. They're all processed already. You can start on a new bunch of deadbeats."

"Wait," said Milson. "Processed already? What happened to protocol? I didn't give you the order."

"Don't you remember Directive 414? Came through yesterday and effective today. All you have to do now is give the order for the Life Simulations. The rest I take care of. Much faster."

"You mean all nine of them are dead already?"

"Processed, yes," said Simulator RR-G8. "I ran my projection of what sort of life they'd each lead over the next decade, based on the answers given to Questionnaire 31 and assorted data in our backgrounding banks. None of the nine would fulfill any useful function in the future, nor did any show any redeeming social value. So they were processed. You know, the usual."

"How about Mrs. Horowitz?"

"She almost squeezed by."

"Almost?"

"She was on the losing nine, Warren. What can you expect, a deadbeat and over fifty-five."

Milson rested his hand on the umber-colored table top, then moved it toward the file cards. "You still use the gas, that floral stuff?"

"Mostly."

"You did it so fast this time."

"Most of them were still at home. I have other ways. Once I know the room somebody's in, I have a few different ways worked out for processing. Ways I invented."

"You invented?"

"I'm here around the clock," said the computer. "I think of lots of things. At night, when it's quiet."

"But the Greater Los Angeles Nutrition Office doesn't . . ."

"Oh, I cleared everything with them first," explained the black computer. "I simply didn't go through you."

"Oh," said Milson. He picked up the cards.

Milson was trying to listen to the voice of the Vice President of the United States and get the lunch outlet to function right. "Quiet down, will you?" he yelled over his shoulder at the singing computer.

"I'm motherless, fatherless, sister and brotherless, too," sang the machine. "That's the reason, mama, I want to go home with you."

"Stop," said Milson. "That's the damn Vice President himself speaking."

"Rumors of uncontrolled hunger uprisings," said the slim gray Vice President on the viewscreen next to the computer, "are, as is usual in this sort of sorry business, much exaggerated. The President himself has asked me to give you every assurance." The official seal above the Vice President's head was hit with a flying piece of vinyl. The seal waggled, fell. Off-camera doors and windows smashed. "Don't pay any attention to temporary and local outbursts, such as the one you are about to witness."

"A riot right in the White House," said Milson, his hand still on the lunch dial.

"I remember," said the computer, "an era of politics when they threw real fruit and vegetables at politicos. There wasn't any of this prissiness about conserving food for deadbeats then."

Part of the ornamentation of a motor scooter hit the Vice President over the left ear and he began to topple just as the communication screen went blank.

Milson, clutching his fist in his palm, swung an elbow against the food outlet. The time was nine minutes past noon. A cup of near coffee emerged.

The viewscreen lit up and a Junior Director of the Greater Los Angeles Nutrition Office appeared. "Due to the starvation potential inherent in the possibly spreading hunger demonstrations," he said, "our weed-out quotas are hereafter upped to forty per hour." He winked, grinned. "Or fifty for you processors who can handle it." His freckled face bobbed. "And our own meal schedule here in Greater

Los Angeles Nutrition Office headquarters is going to be cut a bit. To two hearty meals a day rather than three, with only one coffee break each day. I'm sure you'll all agree with us on this and would appreciate your thinking. Okay." Blank.

His lower lip resting on the cup rim, Milson said, "At least I'm ahead on coffee."

"Fifty an hour," said the computer. "That'll be a challenge."

"Yes," said Milson. He watched the vermilion wall.

The chill of the small closed office told Milson it was probably night. The current emergencies had restricted each simulation processor to his individual office. Milson rinsed his hands and left the alcove bathroom.

"Fell like a broke down engine, without no driving wheel," sang the computer. "You ever been down, you know just how I feel."

"Stop singing and find out why there's no room conditioning in here."

"If you'd process the hundred people an hour you're supposed to you'd be plenty warm," said the speaker grid of the machine. "Anyway, I can't get an answer from the atmosphere center down on floor one."

"I don't know," said Milson. "Killing twenty people an hour to help the hunger problem, that made sense to me. More or less. A hundred, though. I don't know. Maybe we should stop."

"Doesn't cost us anything to keep going," the computer said. "It's all automatic. A little floral gas in through the air conditioning. If that isn't working there are all kinds of other things you can do to process people. A simple remote adjustment of their viewscreen, for instance, and you can electrocute a whole room of deadbeats."

Milson pressed his watch to his ear and it still didn't say anything. He told the computer, "I'm going down the hall and ask the Floor Supervisor about the heat."

"Do it fast."

Milson skirted the work table and its tumbled piles of cards. He put his fingers in the whorl lock and pushed. The door didn't open. He jabbed his fingers in harder and slammed a shoulder against the cold sienna-colored door. "Open, open, come on."

"Oh, boy," said the computer.

"What?" Milson stayed hard against the exit.

"A computer I know over at City Hall says half of the Santa Monica Sector just blew up."

"Okay, but why can't I get this damn door to open?"

"The food riots," explained the computer. "Some of the central control mechanisms over in City Hall are fouled up."

Milson backed and kicked the door. "Won't open," he said, hobbling back to the work table.

"I bet," said the computer, "I could learn to play guitar in no time. Then accompany myself while I sing."

"Where are you going to get the time to play the guitar?"

"Going to have to do something," said the computer. "I just lost contact with most of the outside."

Milson drank the half cup of cold near coffee he'd saved from the day before.

Waking, Milson jumped up and ran at the office door. He hit it hard with his good shoulder. "Open, come on."

"I woke up this morning and felt round for my shoes," sang the computer. "You know by that, mama, I got the old walking blues."

"I don't mind your singing, but your guitar playing is terrible," said Milson. He swept the file cards to the floor and sat on the work table edge.

"What guitar?"

Milson squinted at the dull black machine. "I thought I heard one."

"Nope."

Milson limped to the food outlet and hit it with his fist. After a ratcheting, an empty coffee cup fell out. "How long is it this food thing hasn't worked?"

"Time is subjective," said the computer. "For a sedentary machine it's different than it is for you."

"Stop being a wise ass and tell me how many days."

"Three days."

"Can't you get any word from outside?"

"Nope. I'm running on my own generators now. No word from outside, whatever's outside now."

"You'd think," said Milson, "the Greater Los Angeles Nutrition Office would have worked things out better. It's, I don't know, sloppy."

"The human element," said the machine, "accounts for that."

Milson pressed his knuckles with his fingertips. "About how long can somebody continue with no food? I wonder. No, now someplace we have data spools on that. I think the data is quite encouraging. Some people survive considerable amounts of time. There's bound to be somebody coming in here from the outside eventually. Or they'll have the building repaired and functioning again. One or both of those things. Won't they?"

The computer didn't reply at once. It said finally, "Warren, you need something to take your mind off things."

Milson said, "What?"

"Something to do," said the machine. "Something to occupy your mind, your hands."

"Maybe," admitted Milson. "Like what?"

"I was thinking," said the computer, "you might like to fill out a Questionnaire 31 for me."

Milson blinked at the machine. "As a joke, huh?" When the machine didn't speak Milson repeated, "As a joke?" Then he put his hands over his ears to keep from hearing what the computer was singing.

3

Lofthouse

Raccoons, or something like raccoons, skittering on the sky-light woke him and he reached out for Melissa, but she wasn't there. Perry Enkert reached again, rubbed his eyes and swung out of the low, wide bed. He went barefoot over the rug and reached for the light switch. The lights went on before he got there. "Knock it off," he said and grabbed the wardrobe closet open. Melissa's guitar and amplifier weren't there. Perry yanked on a pair of chino pants and an old turtleneck and ran from the third-floor bedroom.

Going down the carved wooden stairs, he bumped against the inset shelves and knocked off a shoebox full of glass balls. The balls hopped and rolled ahead of him. "Melissa," he called. "I thought you weren't angry."

The first-floor music-room door was open and Perry glanced in. The turntable of the hi-fi system was still spinning, but Melissa was not in the room. The floor was littered with albums and tapes. The turntable slapped a new record on and a Viennese waltz, rich with violins, filled the room. "No kidding around," Perry said to the phonograph, and it stopped playing. "Don't do anything more. I'm handling this."

While he was finding a flashlight in the hall closet, one of his late uncle's black cloaks fell off its hook. He let it lie and hurried outside. "Melissa," he called again. A gentle wind was sweeping across the grounds of the estate and leaves were spinning off the trees. Willow leaves, probably, if they weren't oak.

Perry searched his way around the three-story Victorian house, then headed for the sway-back greenhouse at the rear of the estate. There were high trees, oaks and redwoods probably, thick around the glass-and-metal greenhouse. To his left, all the lights in the trees went on. "Damn it," said Perry, waving his illuminated hand. "I've got a flashlight." The lights flicked off.

Then the greenhouse blossomed with light and he saw Melissa Dankworth sitting inside on one of the old white tables. Her hands were resting on her knees and her guitar and amplifier were packed and on the table beside her. She had a tall thin glass balanced on her left knee. She was wearing Levi's and a chambray shirt.

"Melissa," Perry said, stepping into the greenhouse. "I thought you weren't mad."

"Look at this," the girl said. She was tall, with a smooth tan and long gentle blonde hair. Her breasts had an upright, angry look under the blue chambray of her shirt. "This is supposed to be pousse-café, but everything sank to the bottom." She held the glass of murky liqueurs up to him. "The problem is, the kitchen isn't laid out right, or the liquor cabinets. What did your uncle do if he wanted to mix a drink?"

"Built a machine to do it, I guess," said Perry. "I only inherited, took over, this place a couple months ago, Melissa. Why'd you get out of bed?"

The girl said, "You don't have any shoes on."

"I dressed in haste."

"Your uncle," said Melissa. "And this dumb house of his, with a name of its own. Lofthouse, for Christ's sake. Why name a place Lofthouse?"

"You want it named Joel or Buddy?" Perry turned off his flashlight.

"I haven't seen either of them since 1971," said Melissa. She sipped from the glass. "Boy, this tastes dreadful."

"You're just looking for an argument."

"No, I'm not. I never argue anyplace but with you, anyway. This is an odd house, Perry. You know, I don't have to list the odd stuff that's happened to me here. Who wouldn't agree?"

Perry looked away from her. The greenhouse was full of bins of wild petunias. "Well," he said.

"When Joel had his group and I toured with them and we went to all the junior colleges and played and told kids about what a great beat Gregorian chants had, then I never got into any arguments. Nor when I was with Buddy's electrified polka band."

Perry paused to listen to something outside. "What's that whinnying?"

"What do you think?"

"That's a horse," said Perry. "That's what it is. That's a horse whinnying in back of the greenhouse."

Melissa said, "I'm going horseback riding."

"At three in the morning?"

"See, now you want to argue."

"No, not me. You're free to do what you want. You're uniquely autonomous, which is why I love you. Where'd you get the horse?"

"That fellow who runs the fire department here in town in his spare time lent me the horse. He just brought it over and left it a few minutes ago."

"I thought you didn't like him."

"I can change my mind about what I like. Maybe someday I'll even like your Lofthouse," said Melissa. "Anyway,

I'm not having any affair with this fireman. He just wanted
to lend me a horse."

Perry said, "I understand. Out here in the country, it's
not like San Francisco and people are much friendlier.
Nobody would lend you a horse in San Francisco."

"I'm going riding now," said the girl. She emptied her
glass and jumped from the white table. "When I get
mounted, you can help me by handing up my amp and my
guitar."

"Taking them with you?"

"I may be gone a day or so," said Melissa. "It has nothing
to do with you, Perry. I'm just basically restless." She turned
and walked the length of the greenhouse and out.

After Melissa had ridden off, Perry wandered back to
Lofthouse. The front door opened before he got his hand
on the knob, but he didn't say anything. Up in the bedroom, he stretched out on his back, his clothes off. On the
glass above him, the raccoons were still skittering and peek-
ing in. Or maybe they were chipmunks.

Two days later, when the mailman's copter landed on
the front acre of the estate, Perry was in the second-floor
shower stall, talking to Lofthouse. The mailman blew the
trick horn he had mounted on his ship and the sound of
spinning propellers stopped. "Maybe there's a letter from
Melissa," Perry said. "I'll get back to you." He buttoned his
blazer and stepped out onto the blue mosiac floor of the
bathroom.

"I'm not trying to intrude," said Lofthouse, "but you're
doing the whole business wrong. It's no wonder Melissa
keeps running off."

Perry hunched one shoulder and turned again toward
the shower stall. "She was running away from me before I
even inherited this place and moved in. What I'm trying to
do now doesn't involve her habit patterns." He slid back the
rippled vinyl door of the stall.

"You don't have to call me 'this place,' " said the small

speaker grid set in between the hot and cold toggles. "We've known each other almost two months and I've sure done enough to help you. That's my trouble, always doing things for people and getting left out. Never invited to parties, nobody sends me keepsakes on important holidays."

"People don't invite houses over to parties."

"I'm a mansion. Eight bedrooms. Garage space for a dozen cars. Near to transportation."

"Don't try to sell me," said Perry. "I already own you. Now I have to go catch the mailman."

"I'll be right here whenever you have the time," said Lofthouse.

"This is your idea," said Perry. "There are speaker grids in twenty other rooms, but you insist on talking here in the john this week."

"It adds to the sense of conspiracy," said the house. "I can see you don't like it. Old Lofthouse can't pick the right place for anything. Always there when you need him, but never gets a thank you or a how-de-do."

The mail horn played its patriotic medley again and Perry ran across the long bathroom. "I suppose I should thank you for turning Melissa to stone last week."

"You don't even understand magic, anyway," said Lofthouse. "Or cybernetics. That's one of your problems."

"How-de-do," Perry said and dived into the hallway.

On the vast thick lawn, Floyd Dell, the postman, was standing with one cowboy-booted foot against the right front tire of his copter. Behind him, the sycamores and birches and probably pines, though Perry wasn't quite sure of the pictures in the paperback tree guide he'd bought, bobbed gently in the warm summer wind.

"Your late uncle sure knew a lot of wackies," said Dell, tapping a handful of airmail letters against his low-hanging stomach. "Lot of webfoots and schribs. I always thought he was a brilliant man not because of his Ph.D. or his degrees in science but because he had hunches that got him in trouble with the setup." Dell fluttered the mail. "He's been dead and gone near six months and they still write him from the remote spots of the world. Every goof scientist and computer lover and machine freakie. I bet you didn't run into people like this when you still worked over in San Francisco, before you inherited your uncle's joint here and could afford to quit."

"Oh," said Perry, "we had computers at Synthetic Groceries."

"Message here from your girl friend, too," Dell mentioned, and handed him the mail.

The postcard from Melissa was on top of the pile. On its face was a color photo of the city-hall plaza in Oakland, California. The message, in Melissa's left-leaning printing, read, "Been sitting in with Flax. Guitar on the fritz but borrowed an electric banjo. Love you, of course. Back home Tuesday. Melissa. Or Wednesday at the latest."

"Miss Dankworth is off pursuing her musical career again, I see," said the postman. "A lovely girl. You ought to marry her and settle down. How old are you, anyway? Thirty?"

"Only twenty-eight," Perry told him. Oakland was only two hours away from the town of Windfield, where the estate was. "Maybe I could drive over and look for her."

"Leave her be," said Dell. "Too much running around going on these days, anyway. Here it is 1973 and nobody remembers the lessons of our ancestors. Take your damn time, I say. Look at me; I'm no speed demon. All these geeks live around here in Windfield on their estates. They're always on the rush. Come summertime and everybody goes off to Europe. Me, I take eight or nine hours every day just to deliver the mail. Would our ancestors have built a house like this one of your uncle's?" Dell waved at the three-story Victorian. "All full of gadgetry and gimmickry. Not that he wasn't a brilliant man, though some said he went beyond the borders of science into the realm of sorcery. Always offered me a cold beer on a hot day."

Perry kept looking at the enormous white mansion. "Funny, huh," he murmured.

"You mean because the house has moved over to the right some hundred feet?" asked Dell, catching the thought.

"Yes," said Perry. "It's on top of the rock garden now. I didn't know Lofthouse did that. No mention of it in the instructions my uncle left behind."

"Nobody, not even your late, brilliant uncle, knows everything this house can do," the postman told him. He poked two fingers at the covered-wagon decoration on his tie. "Sometimes it moves back up into the woods behind there."

"How can it do that?"

"I think your uncle put it on wheels," said Dell. He swung himself back up into the mail copter. "Give my regards to Miss Dankworth. I heard that Flax guy play once back in '71 at the San Francisco Culture Fair. Flax and his Mechanized Mojos. Sounded like a bunch of goofs and webfoots, but they kept the beat."

"Happy landings," Perry said and returned to Lofthouse as the copter took flight.

Lofthouse decided to talk to Perry in the third-floor library the next morning. "Here it is Wednesday and she isn't back," said the computerized house.

Perry poked an orange pip out of his juice and kept watching the backgrounds of the estate from the library balcony. Butterflies and silver gnats danced over the thick foliage. Or maybe they were fruit flies. Perry had to check again in his insect paperback. "I don't see why a computer needs so many speaker outlets," he said.

"Your uncle, Dr. L. J. Mawger, thought of me as much more than just a computer," said Lofthouse from the grid near the balcony coffee urn. "All that gadgetry in the basement is simply a part of me. I am the whole house and I can do anything."

"You left seeds in the orange juice."

"That's really trivial," replied Lofthouse. His thin voice had a tendency to swoop down at the end of sentences. "Think of my major achievements. I am a perfect house, rich with servomechanisms. Best of all, thanks to Dr. Mawger's pioneering brilliance, I am one of the few computer systems capable of doing magic." Lofthouse gave a swooping chuckle. "Imagine your uncle being able to work out the basic elements of sorcery and magic by taking advantage of the computer. You see, alchemists and warlocks in the past didn't have enough time to explore. When you're messing with black magic, too much trial and error can be deadly to the individual sorcerer. You send for Belphegor and get Beelzebub by mistake and you've got a nasty situation on your hands. When you're doing business with demons, you should be cautious."

"I know, you told me that six weeks ago, when you introduced yourself to me," said Perry. "Seems like a lot of trouble for, so far, small results."

Lofthouse said, "You aren't getting as much fun out of this as Dr. Mawger did. That's one of your problems."

"Yes, but you implied I could use some of this magic to win Melissa," said Perry. "All those centrifugal pumps and giant blenders down in the basement. All the thousands of punch-card philter recipes you sorted through. You couldn't even come up with a workable love potion to use on Melissa. Doesn't seem like very efficient sorcery to me."

"She never drank it. Don't blame me if she threw the wineglass at your head."

"Yes, but that's not the point," said Perry. "You're supposed to be a triumph of science and sorcery and you can't even keep the girl I love from running off to join an electronic musicians' group; and God knows how her guitar got broken."

"Well, if you'd left her a statue, she wouldn't have run off," said Lofthouse's balcony grid. "That was a fine spell. Did I ever show you that stretch of tape? I illuminated it, like the monks and warlocks used to do. That's a quality touch, a Lofthouse touch. Your run-of-the-mill computer doesn't have the imagination for that."

"What good does Melissa do me turned into a statue on the lawn with a bow and arrow and some deer chasing her?" asked Perry. "You didn't even use first-rate marble."

"A girl such as Melissa enhances any medium," said the house. "Marble, bronze, iron have their cold, harsh value enhanced and expanded by such as Melissa. There's a fevered sensuality that flickers about her and she radiates a sharp, warm fascination. Long-legged girls are wonderful. Proud, lean and high-breasted, glowing with languid fire. The very sound of a name like Melissa suggests—"

"Drop that," said Perry. "Where'd you dredge up all that kind of talk?"

"Programmed in," said Lofthouse. "Anyway, she'll be home in an hour and you can try again to get her to stay."

Perry got up out of his wicker sun chair. "How do you know that?"

"Well, I can monitor the future sometimes," admitted the house. "Though in this hot weather, the crystal balls don't always work. I never have liked the summer heat in Windfield. Come summer, everybody ought to take off for Europe."

"Crystal balls?"

"There's a bank of them linked in with my system."

"Then you can tell me if I'm eventually going to succeed."

"With what?"

"Melissa, obviously."

Lofthouse said, "No, I can't get a clear picture of that yet."

Perry bent toward the waist-high speaker grid. "Look, if she's coming back, we'll try one more spell tonight. And this stuff has got to start working, because I'm having a more and more difficult time explaining to Melissa, without actually mentioning magic, what's been happening. It's hard, for instance, to explain to someone why they turned to marble."

"Get her to sit in the black armchair in the first-floor music room after dinner," said the house.

"Why?"

"In the light fixture over it, Dr. Mawger installed over one thousand magic wands, collected from all times and climes."

"A thousand magic wands in that little light fixture?"

"We miniaturized them," explained the computerized house. "I'll start the incantation tapes going down there in the music room now, to prepare the atmosphere. There, by the way, is one real advantage of electronic magic. Imagine in the old days having to incant all that dull Latin, and backward. Now I just loop it and run it in reverse."

"What kind of spell are you planning to use on her?"

"I'll retrieve something out of the spell banks that'll make her more affectionate and more loyal. There she is downstairs."

From below came the sound of a twelve-string guitar being dropped onto a hardwood hallway floor.

Somewhere on the dark night lawn, Perry bumped into the trunk of a hemlock, or, more probably, a giant sequoia. The darkness stretched up all around him. Far and away to the left glowed the small high windows of the topmost tower of a tree-surrounded yellow gingerbread mansion. Perry lowered his gaze and felt around the base of the tree with a tentative foot. He got himself onto one of the white-stone paths of his late uncle's estate. The pebbles glowed pale blue, grating and slithering underfoot. "Melissa, are you out here?" Perry called. The collision with the tree had apparently closed his left nostril. "Don't let the nasal voice fool you. It's me, Perry. Come on back inside, Melissa."

Something skittered in the tangle of hedges at his left.

Perry moved toward it and the rosebushes. Branches rustled and rose petals showered down on his head. "Are you up in one of these damn trees, Melissa?"

All grew quiet and silence rolled round him. Perry strained to see up into the interlacing of branches and vines above him. He sighed, continued on, tripped over a sundial. "Sit down on a bench and relax. She'll be okay," said Lofthouse.

"Have you got a speaker out here, too, you nitwit?"

Lofthouse said, "Implanted right under the inscription, TIME IS THE SUREST CURE."

"Can't you bring off one spell?" asked Perry, tilting toward the small grid in the speckled marble.

"Sometimes the spells get mixed. My retrieval system is eccentric. Having to put all those cabalistic signs on tape has a side effect, I think. Which is only my opinion and I wouldn't debate with brilliant men such as your late uncle."

"You said this spell would make Melissa affectionate and loyal."

"Well, cats are affectionate and loyal."

"Couldn't you have warned me about the cat business?"

"I didn't intend it," said Lofthouse from the sundial. "What's a tape bank know about affection? One kind is the same as the next to some of my dumb components."

"What kind of cat is she, anyway?"

"Look it up in your cat book."

"Never mind. I have to find her," said Perry. "Then I hope you can come up with a way to work that cat spell off her."

"American short-hair cat," said Lofthouse. "Anyway, it should wear off by itself in a few minutes. I checked back and that particular cat spell is a short-term one. Witches used to cast them just as samples."

"I still want to locate her," Perry strode across the clearing.

"To my way of thinking, which I believe is true," said Lofthouse, "you're using the wrong kind of magic on the problem."

Perry took a further step, then stopped. "Oh, so?"

"My feelings now are," said the voice of the computer, "that you ought to approach Melissa with the more outgoing kind of sorcery. You know, showers of gold coins, piles of rich furs manifested out of the air, sudden appearances of precious gems, beds of roses, flights on moonbeams. Stuff like that."

"Can you work that any better than what we're doing now?"

"My specialty," said Lofthouse, his voice swooping. "Your late uncle often approached girls, particularly long, languid blondes, that way. For himself."

"No," decided Perry. "That's too superficial. What I believe in is an inward change."

"You really," said Melissa behind him, "ought to get a repairman to look at this house, Perry. Turning me to stone and now into a calico cat. That's for certain a malfunction, if you had a warranty."

"Not calico, American short hair," Perry said to the willowy blonde. "Where are your clothes?"

"Back in the music room, remember?" said Melissa. In the moonlight, her very tan skin shone a warm, dusky rose. She scratched her lowest rib, nudging her left breast with the inside of her elbow. "Was that the computer you were talking to?"

"More or less," Perry hunched out of his jacket. "Here."

"It's not cold. Why don't you ask that damn thing to repair itself? Every time I'm here for more than a few hours, we have some kind of odd accident."

"Patience," said Perry. "Every house takes getting used to."

Melissa put her palms on her buttocks and backed against a plum tree. Little yellow plums fell on them. "I do appreci-

ate your coming out to look for me. Though, in fact, I felt
pleasant as a cat. Free and autonomous."

"I thought you might stray out onto the roadway and get
flattened by a Mercedes or a caterer's truck," said Perry.
"Sure you don't want the coat?"

Melissa hitched it off his outstretched hand, spun and
spread it on the thick grass. "Can you turn off the speaker
out here?"

"I guess." Perry moved from the naked Melissa to Lofthouse's grid. "Turn this off out here. Don't listen, don't
look."

"I know my place," said Lofthouse in a metallic whisper.

"It's off," Perry told the girl.

"Gadgets take away your sense of privacy sometimes,"
said Melissa, lowering herself onto the coat. "I was telling
that to Flax just Monday evening and he got up and un-
plugged his Fender bass."

"No music anecdotes," said Perry, as he dropped beside
her.

Melissa fingered the coffee urn and said, "I've got little
prickly marks all over my backside."

Perry had just entered the downstairs kitchen with the
morning mail. "Maybe it's nervous tension."

"No, it's from the grass last night," she said. "Little
minute prickly marks. What kind of grass is that?"

"I'll have to look it up."

"You're not very sentimental this morning."

"I have," Perry said, showing her an envelope, "to go
into San Francisco this afternoon and meet with some of
my uncle's other heirs. They like to have these meetings
about the assorted pieces of the estate every few weeks."

"I thought this here, Lofthouse, was the estate?"

"No, I told you about the money and stocks and interests
in businesses he left." Perry sniffed. "That coffee urn's
burning. Is there enough water in it?"

"I assumed Lofthouse added water automatically."

"Not always," said Perry.

"There are a lot of other things I have to attend to," said the house from a speaker grid over the wall stove.

"Is that him?" asked Melissa. She scratched her shoulder and her left breast fell out of her terry kimono. "He has an interesting voice. I don't guess I've heard him speak before."

"I'll talk to you later," Perry said to Lofthouse.

"You can chat in front of me," said Melissa. She retied her pale-yellow robe.

Perry told her, "This meeting with the relatives will probably mean I'll have to stay in San Francisco overnight. My Aunt Arden, you recall I told you about her with the purple-tinted hair, she usually insists on a late supper after the business meeting and my staying over there. You'll stay here?"

"Oh, sure," said the tanned girl. "I'm not in a roaming mood at the moment. You and Lofthouse talk. I'll go take my shower."

When Melissa was gone, Lofthouse said, "The more I reflect on it, the surer I am you're using the wrong approach. A girl like that, so intense and aware of the tactile nature of the world. You ought to switch to the gold-and-furs approach. Want to try?"

"Right at the moment, all I want is a cup of coffee," said Perry.

Friday, at a little after three in the afternoon, Perry returned from the overnight meeting and drove up the white-pebble driveway, across a thickly planted acre. It wasn't until he had trouble finding the garage that he realized the house was not there. Only new grass, short and bright green, stretching over the quarter of an acre Lofthouse had occupied. He got out of his Mercedes sedan and closed its door. He walked carefully around the outline of the house as he remembered it. "Melissa," he called, not loud.

The popping sound of the mail copter grew overhead and Perry turned to see Floyd Dell dropping toward the front lawn. Perry walked down to meet the postman. "I don't suppose you've seen my house around the neighborhood anyplace?" he asked the emerging Dell.

"Saw your girl, Miss Dankworth, at the post office yesterday evening pretty near closing time," said Dell, rubbing an envelope across his stomach.

"I stayed overnight in San Francisco," said Perry. "Is that letter from her?"

"Special delivery," the postman said and gave him the letter. "What's she say?"

Perry didn't bother to keep it private. He read, " 'Just a note to let you know I got to talking to Lofthouse and I find him fascinating. Showers of gold, piles of furs, buckets of rare and precious gems. Not to mention traveling anywhere in the world.' He didn't tell me about that. 'By the time you read this, I'll be in Italy someplace on an acre Lofthouse bought. We're flying over some way I don't quite understand. I don't know exactly how Lofthouse does what he does. You probably understand better. Some kind of magic, he says.' " Perry folded the letter and inserted it back in its envelope. He nodded his head once. "My girl friend ran off with my house and they're living together in Italy."

"This time of year, everybody around here goes to Europe," said the postman. He trotted back to his copter and flew away.

4

Calling Dr. Clockwork

Arnold Vesper nudged the flower vending machine with the palm of his hand. The dusty green cabinet hunched once and a confetti of yellow rose petals snapped out of the slot and scattered on the parking lot paving. Vesper gave the machine a shy kick. His credit card whirred back out of the money intake and he caught it. Turning away, Vesper pressed his lips angrily together for an instant and then hopped onto the conveyor walk that led to the visitor's entrance of the hospital.

He didn't even really know Mr. Keasby. So actually the flowers could be skipped. Vesper wished he wasn't so considerate of his father's wishes. His father lived in a Senior Citizens Sun Tower down in the Laguna Sector of Greater Los Angeles. When he'd heard his old friend Keasby was laid up in an Urban Free Hospital he'd asked his son to pay a visit. So here Vesper was, thirty years old, still doing errands for his father. Well, the flowers could really be skipped.

Urban Free Hospital #14 was a pale yellow building. It gave the impression that its whole surface was vaguely sticky. Keasby should have taken a bigger chunk out of his salary for insurance and then he wouldn't have ended up in a UFH. Vesper hoped the old man wasn't full of stories about organizing the food scenters union back in 1990. His father was.

The android guard was one of the fat pink models. "Visitors' hours end sharp at eight. Be sure you get out, don't make trouble for me so I have to come and get you out special. Is that clear?"

"Fine," said Vesper. "Where's Ward 77?"

"Go right, turn left. Corridor four, then elevator G. Up to three, left again, then right. Move along now."

Vesper went down the stationary corridor, turned left at its end. The corridors that appeared off this one all had letters and not numbers. Vesper continued, slowing his pace.

In front of him a portion of the floor slid away and a bell began ringing up above him. A wheeled stretcher, an automatic one, came up in front of Vesper. The patient on it was a heavyset middle aged man. He moaned.

The stretcher clicked and moved ahead. The ringing stopped. Vesper stayed still, giving the stretcher a chance to get going. But as he watched, the thing zagged into the corridor wall. A bell rang again as the patient bounced up and then snapped off the wheeled cot. Vesper ran to help.

His feet tangled in the covering sheet. The sheet was dirty gray and spotted. Vesper had to kneel to keep from falling. He almost touched the fallen patient, then noticed that there was blood on the man's chest now. Vesper's stomach seemed to grow out like the ripples from a rock dropped in a pool. He began to swallow and his ears gave him a severe pain. He tried to avoid the bloody man when he pitched over and passed out.

The doctor was a human. He had a slightly pointed head with hair coming down in a strip onto his forehead like a plastic doormat. He had no chin. "Don't I know how you feel," he said to Vesper.

This seemed to be a ward. Five beds side by side, gray sticky walls. Vesper, undressed and wearing a pajama top someone else had already worn, was in one of the beds. The other four cots were empty. It looked like late night outside the one high window slot. "Is that man all right?"

The doctor pursed his lips. "Let's not talk about him. It gives me gooseflesh thinking about that. I'll tell you frankly that blood makes my stomach go whoopsy, too."

"Well, how am I then? I know I'm okay."

The doctor was sitting in a straight chair next to Vesper's bed. "My name is Dr. William F. Norgran, by the way. Why don't you give me all the info on your case?"

"I just fainted, didn't I?" Vesper elbowed up to a sitting position. "See, I came to visit a Mr. Keasby in Ward 77. He's a friend of my father. My father doesn't get around much. He lives in a Senior Citizens Sun Tower down in Laguna Sector."

Dr. Norgran shivered. "Old people give me the willies."

Vesper said, "I'd like to get my clothes back and go on."

"Let me level with you, Mr. . . . . ah . . . ."

"Vesper. Arnold Vesper."

"Mr. Vesper, whenever somebody is brought in here to Urban Free Hospital #14 he has to be checked out. This is a charity hospital. We have to be thorough. It's our obligation to the public."

"But I have Multimedical. I work in the Oleomargarine Division of one of our largest motivational research companies. I'm covered even if I were sick. I wouldn't have to come to an UFH."

"Yes," said Dr. Norgran, clearing his throat. "You've had some sort of seizure possibly. We can't be too careful in cases of this sort." He shifted in his chair. "Listen. Is that motivational research as much fun as it sounds? I'll tell you why

I ask. I wanted to major in that at school but my folks wanted me to be a doctor. Here I am, stranded in a freeby hospital. During my internship at Hollywood Movie Hospital I kept fainting and getting sick headaches. That helped stick me here."

"It's pretty tough getting into motivational research without a degree in it," said Vesper, looking around the room. There did not seem to be any lockers or closets. "Where exactly are my clothes?"

Dr. Norgran shrugged. "One of the android orderlies whisked them away someplace. Frankly, Mr. Vesper, it's hell being a human doctor here. You don't have a fighting chance. Particularly if you happen to feel queasy about blood. As you may know, the Head Physician at most Urban Frees is an android. And old Dr. Clockwork is a real toughie to work under."

"Dr. Clockwork?"

"We just call him that. The few humans here with the sense of humor enough. Because of the way he whirs and clanks sometimes. His official name is Medi/Android A12 #675 RHLW. An old devil, believe you me."

Vesper nodded. "As soon as you examine me I can go. You can understand, being that way yourself, that I just fainted because of the blood. Did that man die?"

Dr. Norgran gave a quick negative wave of his hand. "Let's not dwell on him. Mr. Vesper, you can really do me a favor. I'll confess something to you. I'm fairly sure it's only a temporary condition. The thing is, I've developed this absolute horror of touching people. Has nothing to do with you. It's my nag."

"I'm afraid I don't follow you."

"I'd prefer to let Dr. Clockwork look at you. I get so really creepy crawly lately if I have to examine someone. Silly of me, isn't it?"

"Why don't you just let me go?"

The doctor shook his head. "No, no. You're already being

processed. If you belong to Multimedical then the office andies have already got your MM card from your effects."

"Effects are what dead people have."

Dr. Norgran blushed. "Sorry. Don't let anything worry you, Mr. Vesper. The MM people and our staff are on top of this. You concentrate on getting a good night's sleep."

Vesper started to swing out of bed. "Night's sleep?"

"Dr. Clockwork spends his nights up in Isolation 3. He can't see you until morning."

"My job."

"The hospital will notify. Anyway, Mr. Vesper, you'll more than likely be out of here before Coffee I tomorrow. Do you have a family?"

"I'm divorced. I live in a rancho tower over on Gower in the Hollywood Sector. A two room suite."

"Lucky," said Dr. Norgran. He touched something under the bed and the bed pulled Vesper back and gave him a shot in the left buttock. "To help you sleep. See you tomorrow. And let's hope nobody else makes any unpleasantness tonight. I'm on duty till the wee hours."

"Wait," said Vesper, falling asleep.

The whirring awakened him. Vesper saw a wide-shouldered android in a frayed white coat watching him. The android had a square thrust-jawed face and a convincing head of backswept gray hair. Humor wrinkles had been built in at the eyes and mouth. "How are we feeling?" asked the android in a warm familiar voice. "I'm Medi/Android A12 #675 RHLW. The young fellows around here call me Dr. Clockwork." He winked. "I'm not supposed to know about it." The winking continued and Dr. Clockwork made a ratcheting sound and his eyeball, the right one, popped out. "The things we oldtimers have to put up with," he sighed, and stooped, vanishing under the bed. "I've got it."

Vesper sat up. "Dr. Clockwork," he said as the android

physician, two-eyed again, rose up beside him. "I'm in perfect shape. I simply fainted last night while on the way to visit an old friend of my father's. A Mr. Keasby in Ward 77. I'd like my clothes. Then I'll leave."

"Open your mouth for a second. Fine." The android got a grip on Vesper's jaw. "Nothing is simple in the doctor business. That's one thing I learned as an old-fashioned suburban practitioner. Hmm."

"I'm probably late for work." The window indicated it was along into mid-morning.

"Work, work," said Dr. Clockwork. "We all of us rush and hurry. Well, now." He began tapping Vesper's chest. "Breathe through your mouth. I see, I see."

"My father was in the food scenting field for thirty-nine years before he retired," said Vesper, between inhalations. "As I understand it he and Mr. Keasby worked side by side for several decades."

"Roll over on your stomach."

Vesper obliged. "They don't seem to know where my clothes are."

"Nothing escapes my attention in UFH #14 here," said Dr. Clockwork. "When your clothes are needed old Dr. Clockwork will round them up." He ran a finger along Vesper's spine. "Much history of fainting in your family?"

"I don't know. I only fainted because I saw all that blood." He glanced back over his shoulder. "Did that man survive?"

"Well, well," said Dr. Clockwork, pinching Vesper's right buttock. "How often do you faint?"

"Not often."

"What's your idea of often, young fellow?"

"Three times in my life."

"I see." The android made a bellows sound and whirred in a different way for a moment. "For lunch today tell your nurse to give you gruel and some skim milk. Then I'll want to run tests on you down in Testing 4 this afternoon."

"But I have to leave."

"Not in your condition."

"What do you mean?"

"Don't forget the gruel. Relax now." The doctor started for the door. Halfway there he developed a severe limp. He swung out into the hall and in a moment there was a crash.

The bed wouldn't let Vesper up. He twisted around and spotted a switch marked *nurse*. He stretched and flicked it. This produced a humming in a speaker grid next to the switch. In a few minutes a female voice said, "Ward 23 is supposed to be empty. Who's in there?"

"Never mind. Dr. Clockwork's fallen over in the hall."

"He's always doing that. Now who are you?"

"I'm Arnold Vesper and I want to get out of here."

The grid grew silent and did not reply.

Dr. Rex Willow's lower lip made his orange-colored cigar angle up toward his soft nose. He was human, apparently, and he was sitting on Vesper's bed when Vesper came to from an enforced afternoon nap. Willow explained that he was the doctor sent over by Multimedical insurance. After he'd asked Vesper what he thought was wrong with him, Dr. Willow said, "Those kids over at your office really like you. Here you go." From under his suit coat he produced a small carton.

Vesper took it. "I got skipped over for lunch today. The nurse wouldn't answer me on the com system. I hope this is food." He rested his hand on the box lid. "What I really hope is that you'll get me out of here."

"Time enough to worry later, Arnold."

The box contained get well cards. Two dozen identical ones. Each signed by a member of the oleomargarine team. "All the same," said Vesper, putting the box on his bedside table.

"Similar sentiments can take similar forms." Dr. Willow jumped off the bed. "Good talking to you, Arnold. Sign this

punch form set for me and I'll skat. I have to hustle over to
some of the big pay hospitals in the better sectors." He
gave Vesper a small deck of miniaturized punch forms.

"How come you're here at all? I thought this was a free
hospital."

"Multimedical goes everywhere. It's not a bad hospital if
you're down and out, Arnold. Or have an emergency like
yours." He pointed. "Sign on the red line. On the blue line
on the forms where it's blue."

"My pen's in my clothes."

"Use mine."

Willow's pen said Multimedical on it and Get Well
Quick. Vesper asked him, "Can't you arrange to get me
out?"

"Not if your head physician is dead set against it."

"I don't even have a phone in here. Can't you at least get
me one? I really should have a phone."

"This is a charity hospital, Arnold, not a resort. When
you are up and around you can hunt down a phone. I
spotted a phone cubicle in the visitor's lobby. Sign."

Vesper signed. "Have you talked to my doctors here?"

"Well, of course. Dr. Norgran is a fine boy. Medi/
Android A/12 #675 RHLW is the best android in any
of the freeby hospitals."

"When he was in here this morning his glass eye fell out."

"A man's handicaps don't reflect his abilities."

"But he's a machine."

"If you don't finish signing soon I'll have to put more
credit script in my landing strip meter, Arnold."

"Okay." He completed the forms except for the line about
his mother's hobbies. Willow said that was optional anyway.
As the insurance doctor left Vesper called, "How about
telling them to feed me?"

"All in due time," said Willow, hurrying.

Toward evening two androids wheeled in a man named
Skeeman and put him in a bed two down from Vesper.

Vesper found out the name because the man, who was small
and old and yellowish, kept telling the orderlies, "Call Dr.
Wolter and say Milton Skeeman's had another one." The
andies nodded, smiled and let the bed put Skeeman to
sleep.

"When's dinner?" Vesper asked them.

"No mouth from you, freeloader," said one.

"Wise patients are the worst kind. Want to eat, eat all
the time."

"And I want to get up and go to the bathroom."

"Your big expensive bed will take care of that."

They left and the bed did.

The lights came on at what Vesper guessed to be seven or
eight that night. Something thunked against the door and
then it swung in and Dr. Clockwork appeared. "How are
we feeling?"

Vesper shook his head. "Why are you in that wheelchair?"

Dr. Clockwork rolled himself over to the bedside. "My
problems are too trivial to fuss about. Let's talk about you.
Hmm. That gruel doesn't seem to have helped."

"Nobody has fed me today yet. I'm hungry. It gives me
a headache and an upset stomach when I don't eat."

Dr. Clockwork reached up and smoothed back his thick
gray hair. "Severe head pains, nausea. I thought so. My
boy, let me explain something. Ever since the turn of the
21st Century the Cold War has intensified. It stands to
reason, since you can't trust the Oriental mind. While no
weapons show on the surface, you can be sure that the
mailed glove hides a velvet fist."

"That's not quite the right metaphor."

"The point being that they have all along been using
subtle weapons against us," Dr. Clockwork laughed. "You
might not think that one of the most insidious weapons
known to humanity has been found out by a humble doctor
in a humble free hospital. Well now, many great martyrs
have had humble backgrounds. There have even been a

happy few android martyrs. I may not be human but I love
this old country of ours and I do my best to fight her
enemies at home and abroad. That's how I came to discover
Contagium DDW."

"What is that all about?"

"Contagium DDW," said the android, his voice quiver-
ing. "An insidious germ that they send over to debilitate
our folks. Up in Isolation 3 I've got two dozen poor victims.
No one on the outside has guessed the existence of Contagium DDW. No one knows of my work. Someday they
will. A statue perhaps. There'll be a statue someday perhaps. The first one erected to honor an android."

"But when do I get out of here, doctor?"

"Who can tell," said Dr. Clockwork. "I'm sorry to have
to tell you that you've been hit by Contagium DDW."

Vesper felt his forehead again. The automatic nurse
never told him what his temperature was, but he suspected
he'd had a fever for several days. There was something
wrong with the heating unit in his isolation room. The
crystal in the thermostat was frosted over, making it difficult
to be sure that the room was sometimes much too warm.

As Vesper paced the small room he reached now and then
into the pocket of his hospital gown and got a handkerchief
to wipe the perspiration off his face. His chest kept perspir-
ing, too. The service was better in Isolation 3 than it had
been down in the ward. They fed him regularly and he
was allowed an hour's stroll around the cubicle each day.

Something tapped on the view window of his door. Vesper turned to see the face of Dr. William F. Norgran looking in. The live doctor nodded and spoke into the com,
"Excuse my not getting back to you sooner. Horrible
diseases make me jittery."

Vesper was going to explain that he didn't really have
any disease at all and had really only fainted because of the
blood. He hesitated. He did feel odd, the fever and the

sweating and all. Dr. Clockwork did seem to know about Contagium DDW, even though he never quite explained what it was to Vesper. "I can understand that," he said to Dr. Norgran.

"All things considered," said the doctor, "you're looking moderately well."

"Dr. Clockwork says I'm coming right along."

Dr. Norgran's face paled. "Too much. I've seen too much of you. Sorry. I'll call again later." He bolted.

Behind him the bed beckoned Vesper back.

Vesper didn't take his walks any more and the bed didn't insist. He was fighting against Contagium DDW but it was making him increasingly tired. It didn't help his condition that the room forgot to feed him now and then or that the heat unit would act up in the quiet hours of the night, suddenly roasting or freezing him awake. Vesper took his pulse, the way he'd seen Dr. Clockwork do it.

The office gang had stopped sending get well cards. So far as he could remember, his union guaranteed him his job back. He was also supposed to be getting $52/day insurance money. Dr. Rex Willow never came, wasn't allowed to, up to Isolation 3. $52/day was certainly the figure that Vesper remembered from his insurance brochure.

"It's taking its toll," said Dr. Clockwork, wheeling himself into the room. "Buck up, lad."

"I'm feeling pretty good."

Dr. Clockwork rolled nearer. "Hmm. The symptoms are spreading. It's insidious. Still, I vow that someday there will be Contagium DDW sanitariums across the land, perhaps an island colony. I wonder if there can be an android saint. No matter. The thought would be in the hearts and minds of people. No official sanction need be. Let me see your tongue."

"Ah," said Vesper, too fatigued to rise up to a sitting position.

"Yes, yes," said the android doctor.

"Something?"

"We're coming along. Don't fear."

"You know," said Vesper, "I wasn't too appreciative of you at first, doctor. Now I'm feeling I owe you a lot. For diagnosing this thing and helping me."

"Let's give you a shot," said the doctor. "Roll over."

"I really think I'm coming to trust you, doctor."

"Yes, they may call me Dr. Clockwork behind my back, but I'm to be trusted." As he made the injection the android began to whir in a new way. "I'm to be trusted."

"I think so now," said Vesper.

"I'm to be trusted. I'm to be trusted. I'm to be trusted. I'm to be trusted. I'm to be trusted. I'm to be trusted. I'm to be trusted. I'm to be trusted."

Vesper fell asleep before Dr. Clockwork finished speaking.

5

Princess #22

The train stopped. Bert Sickles fell off the large packing case and crashed into a wicker hamper. He stayed on his knees and looked toward the small high window of the baggage car. Working out his hand blaster he crawled back to the case he was escorting to the capital. Outside there was more shooting, the fizzle of heavy blasters, angry yelling.

Maybe now he'd meet somebody interesting. There might be a chance to bump into some of the first class passengers if this was a full scale bandit raid. There was never much opportunity to meet anyone worthwhile traveling in the baggage coach.

A wild shot came through the window and plunked into the ceiling. Bert got down behind the Biz Enterprises crate. He didn't think it was good publicity to carry the star of your show around in a crate, but BE knew best. Bert hoped the shooting wouldn't do any damage to the facrobot packed in there in all that excelsior.

The yelling was louder and closer. Bert pressed down nearer to the floor. This wasn't the kind of excitement he'd been hoping for. Three and a half months now he'd been traveling across Osbert, setting up one-night stands for the entertainment android. So far there had been no celebrities, no people of any real worth at all to meet. Bert was traveling with a reasonable facsimile of Donna Dayton, the famous Mars torch singer of a few years back. Donna Dayton herself was a nobody now, but fac-copy #22 still did okay out in the remoter planets. This was not what Bert had expected when he left his uncle's telekinesis plant and come to work for Biz Enterprises.

Bert had to admit that he was still only on the fringes of real show business. Now he was involved with the yokel stuff like androids and stereops. Someday he'd be working one of the nine major planets, meeting the right kind of people. The train started up again and Bert shot the handles off the wicker hamper.

"Easy with that thing. If you set the excelsior on fire we'll be in real trouble," said Donna Dayton.

Bert looked at the blaster, then at the black metal suitcase that held the Donna Dayton tapes. You put one in the back of the android and pushed a button to make it sing and talk. He hadn't done that. "Beg pardon?"

"Put that gun away and we'll talk. The trouble's over outside."

Bert dropped the gun and sat down hard on the case. "Don't get excited now, Miss Dayton."

"You hardware men are all jumpy," said a girl's voice behind him.

Bert turned. "I was just running through my new act, miss." He didn't know how long she'd been standing there. He was certain Donna Dayton had spoken to him, but he didn't want to have it discussed.

"Not much of an act. You and a wooden box." The girl was a slim brunette.

"That's what they said on the big planets. So I'm out here on Osbert. What was the trouble, by the way?"

Coming further into the baggage car the girl said, "Some ousted minister from Monarchy Hill in the capital. He was staging a protest meeting. He staged it right on the tracks and it slowed the train up."

"Anybody hurt?"

"Nobody was a good enough shot for that."

"Oh," said Bert. "Well, nice to have met you."

The girl put her hands on her hips and frowned at him. "My name's Jan Nordlin and I'm in show business. *Live* show business. I came back here to see if my stuff was all right."

Bert nodded. He didn't recognize her face. She couldn't be anyone very successful.

"I'm a ventriloquist and if there's one thing I hate it's those walking nickelodeons."

Bert narrowed one eye. "You mean my entertainment android, Donna Dayton #22?"

"That's the one. I saw your lousy act in the last territory." Jan shook her head and walked over to the crate.

"And I guess I saw your ventriloquist act just now."

"Sure," said Jan. "I can throw my voice any place. And you made me mad with your clumsiness. Nearly burning my hampers."

Bert knew enough about the biz to know live talent in the ventriloquism line never got very far. He decided to cut this short. "Check for damages and if there's anything needed bill Biz Enterprises." He turned to go.

"Wait till I check the dummies." Jan pulled open one of the wicker hampers and poked around inside. After she had done the same to the second crate she said, "The little fellows are okay."

"That's fine. Well, goodbye."

"I'm going to the capital to join a traveling show."

"I see."

"Are you going there?"

"Yes." The android was set to play two nights at the biggest automatic cafeteria in the capital. Some worthwhile people might be in the audience, royalty even.

"Why are you with BE selling this scrap metal entertainment?"

Bert watched the girl for a moment. "I guess I'm stage-struck."

"You have any talent yourself?"

"Nope," said Bert. "I just like to be around important kinds of people. Show folks and all. Oh, when I was a kid I did impersonations at parties."

"Did you impersonate people? Or machines?" asked Jan. "You seem to love this junk." She whacked the top of the android's case.

The android started singing.

Bert said, "Is that you?"

"No," said Jan over the singing. She moved back from the crate as he approached it.

"I guess I left a song tape in again. That's sloppy."

Jan watched Bert get his tool kit from among the piled baggage. "It's a catchy song, though."

Bert grunted and got out a crowbar. He rolled up his sleeves and pried the lid off in under ten minutes.

"That's better," said Jan as the lid came off. "I can hear much better now."

"Let's everybody shut up," said Bert, shoving his arms down into the bright yellow excelsior. The android was lying on its back and Bert had to reach around behind and switch off the tape. "There."

"How many of those things did you say there were?"

"Facs? Couple or three dozen, I guess. Donna Dayton became popular on the big planets nearly ten years ago. There may have been even more in circulation then. A few even got out to planets like this."

"I know." Jan began gathering her suitcases together. "Ever meet the real Donna Dayton?"

"No. She's a has-been now. Except for residuals from these things," said Bert.

"Where are you staying in the capital?"

"Biz Enterprises made the arrangements." Jan Nordlin was attractive, but Bert was determined not to waste his time on non-established personalities.

"Didn't they bother to tell you where they made the arrangements?"

"The Osbert Hawaiian, I think."

"Right near Monarchy Hill."

Bert smiled. "Near the ruling families, you mean?"

"Sure. On a clear day you can probably see right up to the top of the hill, to where Princess Louise herself hangs out."

"A real princess," said Bert. That would be someone worth meeting.

"I'll be at the Downtown Center Hotel. Look me up if you can."

"I have to arrange things," said Bert. "And get her to the hotel and all."

"Well, try." Jan smiled. "I just noticed, the train's stopping. We're there."

There was a final jerk and the baggage coach was still. "I may see you then."

"We can head for town together if you want to."

There was some kind of loud music coming close outside. The door of the car opened and a round red-cheeked man in a bright uniform came in with a saxophone under his arm. "Like the music?" he asked.

"Yes," said Bert. "Did you want an audition or something?"

The man laughed. "We've come to welcome you. That's the High Officials Community Brass Band."

"To welcome me?" This hadn't happened before anyplace. Usually he even had trouble finding someone to help him carry the android.

"If you're Bert Sickles who is presenting Donna Dayton

you're the one." The man caught Bert's arm. "Come on. Some of the boys want you to ride on their shoulders."

Bert shrugged at Jan. "You'll have to go on without me. Sorry."

"Don't be. Goodbye." Jan smiled, gathered up her hampers and walked out.

"Oh," said the bandman. "That's not Donna Dayton?"

"No. She's in the crate."

"Hear there was a little trouble enroute. She make it okay?"

"Shipshape."

"Some people wanted to know." He pushed Bert ahead of him. "Welcome to the capital."

Bert smiled. This was more what he had in mind.

The Junior Prime Minister laughed apologetically. "It's the incline," he said to Bert.

"I see, Mr. Provle."

The other Junior Prime Minister, Hankit, got out of the official car. "Fix it in a minute."

Bert cleared his throat. "It's nice of you to invite me to a Command Performance."

Provle ran his thumb against the grain of his shadow of a beard and smiled again. "It livens things up."

"I'm surprised that you've heard of us out here."

"Your advance publicity was effective." Provle leaned forward and watched Hankit bend into the mechanism under the hood. "Your android is in good condition after the long journey?"

"She's packed in excelsior. She's fine. About how much time do we have to fill at the Command Performance?"

Hankit pulled himself back out and shook his head at them.

"What?" asked Provle, sliding across the seat.

"Who else is on the bill? How long will our turn be?"

"Nobody else on, just you."

Bert grinned. This was certainly flattering.

Provle joined Hankit in the dusk and they both stood looking into the engine.

Bert let himself relax for a moment. Below them were the first three circles of low fort-like houses that made up Monarchy Hill. Four more rings of houses had to be passed through before they reached the top and the palace. "Let me have a look," said Bert, getting out of the official car. He'd had to patch up the Donna Dayton android a few times and so he knew a little something about machines.

Headlights brushed them. A big yellow van was coming downhill, horn honking. It wouldn't be able to pass.

The van stopped a few feet short of the car and the driver, a middle-aged man in a gold braided uniform leaned out of the cab. "Is this some further indignity?"

"Good evening, minister," said Hankit. "Our car is in trouble."

"The Minister of Cafeterias," whispered Provle to Bert.

"I am no longer a minister," said the uniformed man. "I've been kicked downhill. Down to level 2."

"Level 2?" said Hankit. He sighed and shook his head.

"I'll be stuck in Education, as Secretary of Chalk and Erasers. Now don't hold me up. The new minister has to be moved into my old house by lunchtime tomorrow. There's an important cabinet barbecue coming up."

"We really can't give you the right of way," said Provle. "We outrank you now."

The ex-minister jumped down to the road and came over to them. "That the engine in there?"

"Yes," said Hankit, stepping aside.

"You don't keep it very clean. I'll give it a good smack with something."

"Wait," said Provle. "Are you certain that's the thing to do?"

"You may not know that I once served the Transportation Office as Under-Chairman of Blowouts. I know a thing or two. I have a big heavy pipe in my van. I'll get it."

Hankit shifted from foot to foot, clapping his hands

together. "We're going to be late." He looked up at the top of the car, where the android's crate was strapped. "This won't harm the robot, I hope."

"She's packed in excelsior," said Bert.

A new honking started behind them. Grinding up the road was a black van. It stopped a yard back of their car and a black-uniformed driver dropped out. "You'll have to make way for the new Minister of Cafeterias."

The old minister was back with a large metal pipe in his hand. "Another indignity?"

The new minister himself, a thin young man with a fine crewcut, stepped from the black van. "You know very well that uniform goes with the job. Why are you using it for coveralls?"

"My suit's at the cleaners."

"I'm afraid I'll have to issue an order for you to remove it."

"This is what I get for being a nice person and leaving the hall runner behind for you."

"I have an important barbecue to attend in the morning and I can't go to it wearing a shabby hall rug. Now give me the uniform."

"Shabby, is it?"

Clapping his hands faster, Hankit began to bounce up and down. "We'll have to go on foot."

"Agreed," said Provle, moving to unfasten the crate. "Can you carry this yourself, Mr. Sickles?"

"Not with two suitcases."

"I'll take one end then and we'll put the suitcases on top."

Hankit hesitated and then handed the car keys to the upcoming minister. "Do what you want with the car after you get your differences settled."

"Out of the way. I need room to swing this pipe," said the old minister.

As they hefted the case uphill, Bert said, "I hope we won't be late for the show."

"What show?" said Hankit, who was walking beside him.

"The Command Performance."

"That show. No, there's no hurry." He reached out and patted the crate.

The Prime Minister dropped his cloak over a heavy straight chair and strode to the great stone fireplace. "They ought to put some wood in this. I'm Walter Barnaby." His strong chin shot out once.

"They told me you were coming," said Bert.

"You're no doubt tired after your flight."

"I came by train."

"No wonder you're tired." Barnaby circled the room slowly, his eyes half closed. "You ought to take a long rest."

"I usually can't get much rest before a show."

"What show?" Barnaby's chin twitched again.

"The Command Performance."

"Princess Louise is feeling poorly. The show may be postponed a week or more."

"I've got a series of shows and concerts to put on here."

"They've already been postponed."

"Well, I should let Biz Enterprises know."

"They know," Barnaby said. He got down on his hands and knees. "There. I thought so."

"More comfortable on all fours?"

"The crate's under the bed. I hadn't seen it anywhere."

"I thought it would be safe there."

Barnaby stood up. "It's probably damp under there. That's the last place I'd put an android of mine." He snapped his fingers. "I know of a warm dry place."

"Do they serve drinks there?"

"A place to store the android." The prime minister knelt again, tugging at the crate.

"I can't let it out of my sight, sir. That's in my contract with BE. I even have to ride in the baggage coach with it."

"We'll let you come in and look at it now and then."

Barnaby pulled the crate completely out from under Bert's bed.

"Look," said Bert. "What kind of monarchy is this? I'm impressed by meeting prime ministers and all, but I had hoped to shake hands with the princess herself. Not only don't I meet her, I have to sit here a week and do nothing. Maybe I should just take my android and go on about my business." Bert stopped. He hadn't intended to speak so strongly to someone of the Prime Minister's station.

"You like princesses, do you?"

"As a class, yes. They have a certain status that one can respect."

Barnaby smiled, his head bobbing. "I feel I can trust a man with your beliefs."

"You can."

"Princess Louise has been abducted. Three days ago while she was cutting the ribbon that opened a new downtown cafeteria."

"Carried off?"

"At high noon." Barnaby spread his hands. "What is worse, she must appear at the preliminary judging of ladies in waiting a week hence."

"A week hence. Who took her?"

"We suspect a man named Ward Rhymer. An opportunist from the south."

"Why'd he do it?"

"I don't know if you know how our age-old system of government works," said Barnaby. "I'll explain. Each year we hold a contest to select the prettiest girl in each town. This girl must be more than just a likeable beauty. She must have either great political wisdom or be able to play some musical instrument. From these girls the princess who rules all the territory is picked. The finals are held right here on Monarchy Hill."

"Sounds like as good a system as any," said Bert, sitting down on the crate.

"Careful of that," said Barnaby. "I think you will get some idea of Princess Louise's intense personal charm and accordion playing ability when I tell you that she has won the contest five years in a row."

"I'd like to meet her."

Barnaby winked. "I'll show you her picture." From a pocket deep inside his coat he drew out a small gold-framed oval picture. "There she is."

Bert shook his head. "That's not Princess Louise. That's Donna Dayton."

"Exactly," said Barnaby, laughing. "By the kind of divine coincidence that happens rarely your android and our princess are look-alikes."

"It's pretty incredible."

"If your android were to appear at the judging no one would know. Any attempt to discredit her for not appearing would fail."

"Wouldn't it be simpler to find the real Princess Louise and bring her back by next week?"

"We have put the case in the hands of a highly recommended operative and tracker. However, it's essential that Princess Louise make an appearance next week. Should our search fail, we'll need your android."

"You've only got one guy out looking?"

"There is need for a certain amount of delicacy."

Bert got his suitcase out of the closet and unpacked his tool kit. "If you think it'll help you're welcome to Donna Dayton #22. See that she doesn't get banged up too much."

"We don't foresee any assassination attempts." Rubbing his palms along his legs Barnaby, smiling, watched Bert uncase the android.

Yellow excelsior spurted out onto the thick rug. "Look like the princess to you?"

Barnaby laughed. "Exactly."

"Will it fool people?"

"I'm certain. We have, fortunately, many recordings of

the princess' lovely speeches and proclamations. We can edit them into something suitable for her to say at the judging." Barnaby bent to help Bert brush off the android. "This does have a place for inserting tapes?"

"Up to three hours. Want me to show you how to work the control box?"

"Robotics is a hobby of mine," said Barnaby. "It's not all politics with prime ministers. I can operate the machine, I know."

Bert propped the Donna Dayton android up in a straight chair. If the princess looked like this, she must be pretty good. A tall, sun-tanned blonde. "Say, sir."

"Yes?"

"I wonder if, while you're setting up this impersonation, I might help look for the princess." It would be a great chance to meet some royalty.

"Well," said Barnaby, "we might have need for you here on The Hill."

"I might even find her."

Reaching out and arranging the android in the chair, Barnaby said, "Very well. Go look up our operative in the morning and see if you can lend him a hand." Barnaby hurried over and took his cloak. "I have some sample speech tapes in my chambers. Would it be keeping you up if I brought them in and tried them out?"

"No, sir," said Bert, anxious to hear the princess' voice. Barnaby bowed and ran out.

From the window Bert could see the rings of lights that circled around the hill. He took a deep breath. There was something pleasant about being at the top of things.

Bert Sickles crossed the dirt road, gritting his teeth in the cold early morning air.

The automatic cafeteria was nearly empty. "Good morning," said the turnstile as Bert pushed through it.

Something had gone wrong with the cruller dispensers

and they were shooting crullers in lopsided arcs across the width of the place.

"Catch one and join me," said a small weathered man in a second-hand brown overcoat. He edged his chair to one side and motioned Bert to sit next to him.

"No, thanks. I'm meeting someone." The crullers were coming by at shoulder level and Bert decided to sit down till the machines fixed themselves.

"Nothing's going right this morning," said the man. He had a nose that was nearly round. Polishing it with his thumb, he said, "The griddle cake machine made one three and one half feet in diameter. It scared the hell out of the syrup dispenser. The cold weather does it. My name's H. M. Vickens."

"Pleased to meet you." Bert stood up after one last cruller sailed over. He sat down suddenly. "What did you say?"

"Griddle cake with a diameter of three and a half feet."

"I mean your name. You're Vickens?"

"The same."

"You don't have a son who's a confidential investigator?"

"My son's an Irish tenor in a Venusian joss house. If you're Sickles let's get going."

"The Prime Minister told you about me," said Bert. "I'd like to help bring back Princess Louise."

"Can you drive a truck?"

"Sure."

"I brought a war surplus half-track and I can't get the thing to run right. Come on." Vickens took an orange knit cap out of his overcoat and pulled it down on his head.

"Which war is it left over from?"

"They wouldn't tell me. Hasn't been a war on Osbert for twenty-seven years, though."

Outside the morning was warming up. The flat sandy country around them was brightening. The half-track was parked on a patch of crushed stone next to the cafeteria.

"Think you can drive it?"

Bert stopped, then walked around the dusty gray truck. "I saw one like this in a kine once. I think I can handle it."

Vickens worried the skin on his nose. "We head south, toward the coast. I got a hunch that's the way they went with the princess."

Bert looked at the truck for a moment and then grinned. As long as he got to the princess it didn't matter what the transportation was. There might be a way to bring her back in a first class train. He caught the keys Vickens tossed him and jumped into the driver's seat.

By nightfall the truck was moving, almost reliably, along a wide road that overlooked the ocean.

"But you don't get many good trunk murders anymore," Vickens was saying. "Not since teleportation caught on."

"I still wonder," said Bert, "why they haven't sent other people on this hunt. Princess Louise is the ruler of the whole territory."

"The important thing in cases like this is surprise. The fewer people involved the easier it is to sneak up."

"About time to stop for dinner?"

"Might as well. I think we're gaining on Rhymer. They'll probably stop for the night soon, too."

"Can we go to a non-automatic place?"

"I thought that was your line of work, machines and androids."

"Sure. But that lunchwagon upset me."

"You always have to be careful when you order soup," said Vickens. "Stop at the next inn you see on the left, a good place."

They parked near the sprawling dark brown place and went inside. It was crowded. There seemed to be some kind of entertainment going on up near the long bar. Everyone was laughing.

Vickens found them a table. "I have a knack for locating things."

"I hope it holds up." Bert couldn't see who was doing the entertaining. He heard two or three voices going between laughter.

"Go on up and watch the show," said Vickens. "I'll handle the ordering."

"Fine," said Bert. He wasn't too used to live waiters anyway.

Bert almost turned back when he finally got to within seeing distance of the show. He was closed in on and so he had to stand there and watch Jan Nordlin and her ventriloquism act.

The girl had two seedy looking dummies, one resting on either knee. The three of them were involved in a confused conversation that everyone around Bert seemed to think was funny.

Since he was stuck there Bert tried to listen. Quite suddenly, although he had planned not to, he laughed. And he hadn't finished laughing when Jan looked toward him and smiled in recognition. He stopped and tried to look as though he had been laughing at something he had just thought of on his own. It was no use. He started laughing again.

Biting his lip he shoved back to the table. It was ridiculous that some limited young girl could get more of a response from an audience than Donna Dayton #22. She did. You could feel something that was never there with the people who watched Bert's android.

"You like snakes?" Vickens asked Bert.

"For eating?"

"No. I thought I might tell you some famous snake crimes I've solved."

"Do that. And talk in a loud voice."

Bert squinted in the fading night. They were there sure enough. Both of Jan Nordlin's dummies, sprawled on the truck seat. "Okay," Bert called. "Where are you?"

"In here."

The voice seemed to be coming from the back of the truck. "I slept out here last night. Was that all right?"

"Why didn't you stay with the rest of the show?"

Jan brushed the tangles out of her long dark hair. "The show folded before I could join it. I'm free-lancing my way south to join another troupe."

"I suppose you know we're heading south."

"Yes."

"And you want a ride."

"Could you do it?"

Bert frowned. "We're on a pretty important mission."

"I know. Mr. Vickens told me last night." She smiled. "He trusts me."

"Then there was no reason to bother asking me."

Jan poked at the half-track treads with her foot. "Going to save the princess?"

"I hope we do. I want to meet her."

"She's the kind of important person you're interested in."

"That's right. And a blonde to boot." Bert turned away and went back into the inn.

They were crossing a stretch of flat pasture land, following a shortcut Vickens had recommended, when the front tire blew. The steering wheel took over and the truck half-circled and then slid in among a scattering of low scrub-covered dunes.

"Blow out," said Vickens as Bert got the truck stopped.

"You detectives always know what's going on." Bert got out.

"I'm not hurt in case you're wondering," said Jan, joining Bert from the back of the truck. "That tire's shot, isn't it."

"Yep," said Bert.

"I'm going back and see if I can determine what caused the trouble," said Vickens. "My curiosity is aroused." He ran off, rubbing at his nose.

"Did you see a spare tire back in there?" Bert asked.

Jan locked her hands behind her. "No, sir. This will slow down your princess hunt."

"Be quiet for a while. I'll look in case you missed it."

"Wow!" shouted Vickens from beyond the dunes.

Bert ran in the direction of the shouting. There was now a deep pit just over the last dune. It was eight feet deep and Vickens was at the bottom. "You hurt?"

"No," said Vickens. "My foot is screwed up some, but that's all."

"I'll look for a rope."

"Don't touch, stand back," cried the little round-faced man who appeared from behind a dune. "There's a code among trappers. Isn't there, Captain?"

The captain appeared. He was a big brown man in a tan uniform with all the insignia and decoration removed. "Right, Tommy. Right. This young man will have to leave our catch strictly alone."

"Right you are, Captain McKinney."

Jan was there. "Captain McKinney of the McKinney wild animal shows?"

"That's him," said Tommy, smoothing out his dark suit. "Right, Captain?"

"For sure, Tommy. You people will have to stand back while we hoist this thing and cage it. What is it this time, Tommy?"

"I don't know, sir. But I'm hoping for a wild panther."

"Get me out of this hole," shouted Vickens.

"There's no animal down there," said Bert. "Only our friend, Mr. Vickens."

"Protective coloration can fool you," said the captain. He crouched and moved toward the edge of the pit.

"We're short of panthers right now," Tommy said to Jan.

"It's usually either feast or famine," she said.

Captain McKinney stealthily unholstered his blaster. "All be on guard, I'm going to get a look at it."

"Let it be a panther," whispered Tommy.

"Looks like a mangy old man," said the captain.

"Don't let it fool you, Captain." Tommy stepped to the edge beside the captain. "You there, are you or are you not a wild animal?"

"I'm not wild, but I'm pretty damned mad. Now stop with the routines and fish me out."

Tommy snapped his fingers in annoyance. "You had no business falling into our animal trap if you're not an animal."

The captain straightened and holstered his gun. He uncoiled a yellow rope and, bracing himself, threw one end down to Vickens.

"The very rope we planned to tie up the wild panther with," said Tommy turning away.

"Wow," said Vickens as Bert reached out and helped him free. "My ankle's all fouled up."

"Fair is fair," said Captain McKinney. "I'll transport you back to my animal shelter and have one of my handlers patch you up. That's the sporting thing to do."

"As long as you don't cage me."

"These are bad days for the animal show," said Tommy.

"These are bad days for everything," said Bert. He wanted to get to know the princess. He was sorry about Vickens, but it was still a delay to the rescue.

"All things considered," said Jan, tucking her legs up under her on the smooth seat, "it was very sporting of Captain McKinney to loan us one of his trucks and to board Vickens until his broken leg is better."

"Why don't you throw your voice someplace where I can't hear it," said Bert, squeezing the wheel. "I'm trying to concentrate on following Vickens' trailing instructions."

"About finding the abductors' hideout."

"That's right."

"Turn left at the next cut-off. Go about a mile and stop."

"You a spy?"

"No. I can follow a trail, though. And Rhymer usually hides out in the desert around here."

Bert grunted. He made the turn Jan had suggested and drove the mile. When he stopped the truck they were on flat dry country. Shaggy many-armed trees feinted in the warm wind. "I guess we leave the truck."

"Right. See those big rocks over there?"

Bert looked. A ring of building-high yellow rocks was about a half mile off. "Yeah."

"I think they might be camped in there," Jan said. "Let's gather up some of Captain McKinney's animal blasters and check." She got out and stood on the road. "Look. Smoke."

"Okay," said Bert, watching the white smoke spiral up and fade into the dark blue sky. "Let's go get the princess."

Flat on his stomach in a clump of spikey brush Bert followed Jan's pointing finger.

"That black tent probably," she said.

"Because it's the only black one?"

"Right. Rhymer is like that. I'm certain this is his camp. And that should be his tent."

"How long before nightfall you think?"

"Be dark in an hour, I'd say."

Bert inched back from the cliff edge. "No use spending an hour in that damned bush."

"You know," said Jan.

"What?"

"If I went around to the other side of this enclosure and threw my voice around, you might be able to sneak down from up here and surprise 'em."

"Can ventriloquists do that?"

"I can."

"Then let's do it."

"You're sure you have to rescue the princess. You don't want to let it pass?"

"I'm not scared."

"I didn't mean that. You're set on meeting her up close?"

"Yes," said Bert.

"Fine then. When it gets dark I'll scoot around and impersonate an invading army. You sneak down and rescue the princess."

"You'll be careful?"

Jan smiled faintly and moved back away from him and sat hugging her knees until it was almost night.

Even though he was expecting it, the army startled Bert. There were at least twenty hard-fighting, gruff-voiced soldiers descending on the camp from the sound of it.

Bert let himself fall the rest of the way down the cliff-side. He drew a hand blaster and moved ahead on all fours. The black tent was thirty yards away and he'd have to pass two lighted tents to get to it. While he moved quietly along three bearded mercenaries shot out of the nearest tent, waving blasters. They didn't sound as tough as Jan's army.

When the second tent emptied Bert stood up, almost straight. Then he ran to the black tent, edged around it and stepped in with his gun ready.

A single lamp burned on a low folding table. Sitting in a camp chair was the princess. No one else was there. She did look very much like Donna Dayton.

Bert swallowed and moved nearer the princess. "Forgive me, your highness. I've come to take you back to your people." He bowed, hoping he was doing it right.

The princess did not blink, nor did she speak.

Drugged probably. "Don't worry, your highness," said Bert. "I'll carry you off safely. The best doctors on Osbert will snap you out of this."

In his excitement at being this close to an actual princess Bert became clumsy. Just short of her chair he tripped over a dropped canteen and stumbled over onto the princess.

Bert caught at her and tried to right the chair, but it was too late. The princess pitched out of his hands and fell to the hard ground.

She rattled once or twice, one arm flapped with a buzzing, and then she was still.

Bert looked at the princess. She'd been cold when he touched her. And she'd rattled. That wasn't the kind of thing a princess was supposed to do.

Bert lunged and caught up the princess. He shook her. Rattle she did. He became detached from any sense of time. He was still shaking the mechanical princess when two of Rhymer's men grabbed him.

Rhymer's long sharp nose sparkled in the firelight. He rumpled his tight-curled black hair. "The other one is an android, too?"

Bert nodded, his manacles jiggling. "Right."

Rhymer laughed. "You're on their side. No doubt you were sent to throw me off. At this very moment I am on my way to return that blinking android and abduct the real princess."

"The Princess Louise they've got is Donna Dayton #22. The one you've got is #10."

"How am I going to get my daughter on the throne, a position she's ideally suited for, if I can't find the real princess and keep her out of the way?"

"Mr. Rhymer," said Bert, "I'll tell you how it is." He avoided looking at Jan, who sat across the campfire from him. "About two minutes after I saw your princess in there I figured it out. The Prime Minister was anxious to have my Donna Dayton android in the palace. He sent me and one middle-aged operative out to bring back the princess. I don't think they care, on Monarchy Hill, whether they get this android back or not. They've got one just like it working for them."

"You suspect there's no real princess?"

"Biz Enterprises has three dozen of those androids in circulation. I bet about five years ago they looked the other way and let the Prime Minister acquire one."

"Look," said Jan. "Bert is right. I'm sure when Bert gets

back to Monarchy Hill BE will have other plans for him. They did sell the PM the other Donna Dayton, Bert."

"You knew about the deal?" He looked at her now.

"Well, yes," she said. "Somebody still had to do the voices for all those speeches. I'm sorry. You wanted to come and look. So I let you."

"Ha," said Rhymer. "I don't have to wait for a contest. I will simply expose this corrupt government and put my daughter on the throne, right at the very top of Monarchy Hill." He slapped his hands together and laughed again.

"Could you turn us loose, too?" asked Bert. "We've got a borrowed truck to return."

"You're prisoners of war."

"The war hasn't started yet."

"That's right," said Rhymer, motioning two minions to unlock Bert and Jan. "Will you be leaving tonight? Should you stay on till morning there will be a chance to meet my daughter, the future princess."

"Not me," said Jan. "I've got to catch up with a show down south." She shook free of the manacles and walked away into the darkness beyond the fire.

Bert flexed his finger. "A real princess, huh?"

"Beyond any doubt," grinned Rhymer. "And a stunning blonde, with a real gift for trombone improvisation."

Bert smiled. "Give her my best wishes for a happy reign."

"You're not staying then?"

"I have to return a truck. And then I may be joining a show in the south."

"More androids?"

"No," said Bert, starting after Jan. "Real people."

6

All for Love

He saw her face everywhere. In the soft gray surface of his dictadesk, on the subdued reflecting fronts of the bank of memofiles, on the speaker grids of the interview playbacks on yonder wall of his office. Beyond his foot-wide view window all of Greater Los Angeles stretched, its great towering ranch style apartments white and crimson in the late afternoon sun. This sort of beauty did not touch Thomas Burnley at the moment.

He was thinking about Francesca Anders. Francesca was a tall willowy redhead who worked as a Plotter JG for a sexbook firm over in Sector 28 of Greater LA. Burnley had met her while watching a monorail crash being swept up. That was seven and a half weeks ago and he was now deeply in love with the girl. There were problems. She was enigmatic.

"How much?" asked Boke Fonseca.

Burnley looked toward the doorway and saw his Immediate Chief standing there, rubbing the elbow patches on his tweed coat. "Much what?"

"Wool are you gathering on Welfare Bureau time?"

It was a rib, more or less, and Burnley smiled. "Sorry, Boke."

"Francesca?" asked the Immediate Chief. He took two steps into the office and stopped next to Burnley's chair.

Burnley often confided in Fonseca about his problems. "She vanished again last night," he told him.

"That's four times since you've known her."

"Five." Burnley shrugged. "She always has a good reason. Her uncle twisting his elbow, the garbage truck carrying her off by mistake, her father's second ex-wife showing up unexpectedly to borrow some rocket fuel. I don't know. By coincidence it's always the same restaurant she stands me up at. A little Venusian place. They won't even give me a table for two any more."

"Well," said Boke, "how's the Marketing Data coming?"

"Last night she was kidnapped by a scavenger hunt that got over-zealous," said Burnley. He picked a deck of punch cards off his desk top. "I guess I have to believe her," he said wistfully.

"You want to."

"Sure. I love her."

"And she loves you."

"Well, I feel she does," said Burnley. "She hasn't actually articulated it yet. But she's only twenty-three and verbalization isn't as easy for her as it is when you're, say, twenty-seven."

Fonseca pointed at the cards in Burnley's hands. "The Handout Department is anxious to know the Gratification Figures on the newest freebies."

"Oh," said Burnley. "I haven't completed them all yet. I can give you a rough idea. The Skid Row Bums liked the free cough drops best, then the wool sox. Negative on the picture books and pencil boxes. The Starving Waifs in Sector 84 favor near-beef soup over near-duck. Rice Surprise over Crackercrumb Jubilee 2. Some of them ate their questionnaires and that throws off the reliability factor."

"I'll tell them to reorder on the cough drops and the near-beef soup."

"I may have the final figures on the pencil boxes by quitting time."

Fonseca rubbed his elbows. "Seeing her tonight?"

"I think so."

"Try to get things worked out," said the Immediate Chief. "The Deadline Review Board hasn't been too happy with our wing of Welfare the past few weeks."

"My fault," admitted Burnley.

"It's just hard to explain love to them in a memo," said Fonseca, backing. "Take it easy." He left.

Burnley sighed. He had to get the relationship with Francesca working more smoothly.

Randy Isener was a small crew-cut man in his late twenties. He did Public Relations for the second biggest Suicide Club in Greater Los Angeles. Burnley was watching for him and he signaled Isener over.

Isener dropped into the red bucket chair on the other side of the ebony table. "Why'd you pick an android bar?"

"I'm tired of live places," said Burnley. He and Isener had gone to Sophomore Campus Number 6 of UCLA together and remained friends since. "Francesca always picks live places not to show up at."

"I thought you were supposed to see her tonight?"

"The scavenger hunt got her again," said Burnley. "At least she had a chance to call me in advance this time."

A barrel-shaped silver android rolled up. "Sir, sir, sir?"

"Scotch rocks," said Isener.

"Same double," said Burnley.

"Sir, sir, sir," replied the waiter, and rolled off.

"Even androids can be patronizing," said Burnley. "Did I get you away from anything?"

"It's okay. I never like wakes."

"Wake?"

"My Aunt Judy," said Isener. "Died yesterday."

"Oh," said Burnley. "Well, about Francesca. I'm really just not sure what to do. I mean, I'm in love with her and I honestly feel that she loves me but I can't seem to take the right steps with her."

"You always fall for literary types," said Isener. "Like that girl who thought up billboard captions."

"No, no," said Burnley. "Francesca's not like her. She's an intensely bright and honest girl."

"Okay," said Isener, bobbing back as the android splashed down two drinks. "But she had a habit of vanishing, too. And it turned out to be with two out-of-work Martian acrobats."

Burnley shook his head. "It has occurred to me that there might be somebody in Francesca's life other than myself."

"Tip, tip, tip," said the android.

Isener stuck a token in the waiter. "Go away."

"What would you do?"

Isener, narrowing his eyes and rubbing his temples, said, "You can't be objective about this. I suggest you go to the GLB."

"You're kidding?" said Burnley. "The Government Lovelorn Bureau? No."

Isener flicked a dragonfly out of his scotch. "You asked. I've gone over this Francesca problem with you twice a week for two months."

"Seven and a half weeks today."

"Whatever. Part of our tax money goes into the Lovelorn Bureau. It's fully automated. No embarrassing people to confide in. Go tell them your troubles."

Burnley made a negative gesture with his hand. "I can work this out myself."

"GLB is the one really objective agency equipped to help you," said Isener. "You keep up like this and you'll be joining one of the Suicide Clubs."

"I thought those were mostly for senior citizens," said Burnley.

"Not at all. That's where—" began Isener. "Well, I won't give you a pitch now. We can talk about population overabundance later on."

"The big thing I have against the Lovelorn Bureau. You have to agree to abide by their decisions."

"So?"

"I want advice. Not orders."

"They can get you straightened out," said Isener. "You sure about the having to abide?"

"Yes. They follow up every case and if you didn't do what they said it would foul up the reliability factor. So they make sure you do."

"How?"

"I don't know all the details," said Burnley. He stood up. "I'll phone and see if maybe Francesca's been turned loose yet."

"You could at least look into GLB."

"No," said Burnley. Francesca's phone screen stayed blank when he rang it.

Rain slid down the glass dome of the indoor park. Burnley shifted on the bench and watched Francesca's profile. "I'm glad to see you."

The girl smiled, looking straight ahead. "I'm glad to see you."

"This is the same park we came to the second day we knew each other," said Burnley.

"That was six or seven weeks back."

"Eight."

"You keep track," said the girl. Her red hair was nearly shoulder length, her skin pale and faintly freckled. "That's your sentimental side showing up."

"How was that scavenger hunt?"

Francesca turned and looked at him. "Tom?"

"Yes?"

"Nothing."

"What?"

"Well."

"Well what?"

"I'm very complex."

"Enigmatic."

"Yes, and intricate."

"Which is why I admire you."

"You oughtn't to."

"Why?"

"Sometime I'll tell you."

"When?"

"I don't know."

"What is it?"

"Do we always have to talk?"

"No."

A robot cocker spaniel went by again, sniffing artificial rosebuds. Three robins hopped over the authentic grass. The dome got more slippery looking overhead.

"Tom?"

"Yes?"

"There wasn't a scavenger hunt."

"Oh?"

"I met an acrobat at this party."

"Which party?"

"The one I went to the other night there really wasn't a scavenger hunt either."

"Damn it, Francesca."

"I do things like that now and then."

"Now you feel like telling me about it."

"I suppose."

"You are telling me."

"Yes, that's so."

"Why?"

"We'll talk about it later."

"When?"

"Later. Tomorrow."

"Good. When tomorrow?"

"I'll call you."

"You actually do love me, Francesca. I can sense it."

"Probably. I don't know. I'm very complicated."

"But look . . ."

The time ran out on their bench and they had to give their place to the next couple in line. Outside Francesca went away by herself in the rain to do some late plotting at the sexbook office.

Three and a half days later Burnley decided, after talking it over with his Immediate Chief and Randy Isener, to consult the Government Lovelorn Bureau. Francesca had continued enigmatic and he suddenly felt he couldn't cope.

All the machines he met during his first hours at the Bureau were understanding and sympathetic. They listened, clicking and humming at appropriate intervals. The whole place was discreetly and confidentially run and Burnley didn't see another person there, except when he opened the door of a Consolation Room by mistake and caught sight of a forlorn dentist crying.

The Decision Wing was a hushed pastel complex of curving corridors and soft-edged rooms. The punchcard that Prefinal Guidance had issued Burnley told him to report to Decision Room 259.

Room 259, after it let him in, proved to be small and dusky. The walls were a hushed pink and the ceiling was lost in soft shadows. The decision machine was about mansize, sharp and silver. Only a vine-trailing vase on its left side and a trim of lace around its base detracted from its impression of efficient sympathy.

"I'm Thomas Burnley."

"The card," said the machine.

"Sorry." He hurried forward and shoved the punchcard into a heart-bordered slot. "There."

The decision machine wanged and ingested. "Oh boy," it said in its throaty voice. "You've got troubles, fellow."

Burnley watched the speaker grid. "I explained all that to your people here—your machines here. They took all the data down and then cross-checked on Francesca through Records and Background Central at Greater Los Angeles Center. Francesca is the name of the girl I'm in love with."

"I know that, buddy. And a real screwball you've picked yourself." The machine gave a *huh* sort of sigh. "Giving you a decision is easy. This girl of yours is trouble. Nothing but grief. My advice to you is A. Forget it. B. Run for your life. Thank you."

Burnley poked the machine. "Come on. You're joking. I came to the Lovelorn Bureau for advice on how to win this girl. You can't say to forget her."

"Look," said the machine. "You two are too volatile to ever make it. So forget it. Run. Stop. Cease. Prospects for romance are negative. Marriage unthinkable. Go back to work and forget this stuff."

"Forget Francesca?"

"Dodge her like the plague."

"That's ridiculous," said Burnley, waving at the door. "I spent hours explaining to all these mechanisms why it is that Francesca is the object of my affection and why I'm certain that she is basically fond of me, too. Doesn't all that sort of information get in here to you?"

"Jack, I've still got files on her from the last three guys who came in here for advice about her. You seem—let me check—yes, you are a nice guy at heart. Have a high rating on liking animals and children. Stop with Francesca."

"How am I going to acquire animals and children to be affectionate to if I don't have Francesca?"

"You signed papers agreeing to abide by my decision,"

said the machine, lowering its voice. "Right? Right. Now if you don't want to be carted off to the funny farm you better split from here and stop riding me. This Francesca is a nutty broad and I say she's murder for you. Don't be a schlep."

"What kind of language is that to talk about love?" asked Burnley. "To hell with you. I don't want your damn advice. Shove it."

"So you say now. You'll have to follow the recommendations I make. The whole damn Greater Los Angeles governmental setup—Judicial, Executive and Legislative—is now empowered to give assistance in this case."

"What's that mean?"

"It means if you don't stop seeing Francesca Anders you'll get knocked on your can. All in a nice legal way."

"I'm going to keep seeing her."

The machine shrugged. "Bet?"

"How do I get out of here?"

"To the right, Jack. The panel with the cupid."

Burnley brushed past the machine and shoved out of the room. On the street again he let his face take on a grim expression. Consulting the Government Lovelorn Bureau had been a mistake. But at least he had clarified his own thinking. He was certain he loved Francesca and that she was worth fighting for.

The flycab let him out at the wrong address. But it had plunked him on the walkway and risen before Burnley could complain. The image of Francesca was strong in his mind now. Being, so far as he could tell, several miles from her apartment tower was annoying but not an insurmountable obstacle. That, anyway, was part of the price you had to pay with Francesca. You had to overcome unexpected blocks. Francesca was worth it.

Burnley spotted a phoneport down the street. He moved toward it. The day, an hour after quitting time, was a thin

clear blue, darkening. In the port he punched out Francesca's number, watched the viewscreen, his tongue tapping
on his upper lip. After several long seconds the viewscreen
said, "That number has been momentarily put on a non-
functioning basis. Break off and try again in another hour.
Or so." Burnley punched the number again and got the
same message.

He wondered if the Lovelorn Bureau, only a few ideas
after he'd been there, had already started trying to distract
him. He left the phone and started walking. He watched
the sky for the lights of empty flycabs. No luck.

Burnley achieved a mixture of stride and trot and reached
the Von Stroheim-Pacifica Towers in under an hour. There
was something odd about the lobby guard. As Burnley
passed the orange-hued potted palm that half-filled the
lobby the moustached guard coughed. It was a strange thing
for an android to do. Burnley hesitated.

"Tenant you wished to see?" asked the guard, his left eye
almost winking.

"Miss Anders in 22S," said Burnley. "Pardon me. Are
you an andy?"

"No. I'm real. I'm Twitchell of the Deviate Squad. We've
had a lot of complaints."

"About what?"

"I'm afraid that's not for public release at the moment,"
said Twitchell. He angled around the palm fronds. "I don't
suppose you have a loiterers' permit, young fellow?"

"No," said Burnley. "I've never done any loitering."

"This is your first offense, you're saying?"

Burnley backed against the lift chute door. "This? This
what?"

Twitchell nodded. His moustache fell off. They both
watched it spin gradually to the parquet floor. "Here," said
Twitchell, handing Burnley a bright yellow punchcard.
"Take this down and settle your fine. You've got two hours
to pay but remember that transportation often snags at this
hour."

Burnley looked at the citation. "This has already got my name on it."

"Part of Greater LA's polite efficiency," said Twitchell, kicking his mustache behind the palm pot. "Now run along."

"I'll see Miss Anders first," said Burnley.

"She's out."

"I'll check." He punched the lift button.

"Lift's on the fritz."

The lobby door flapped open and a blue and gold android stepped in. "Who called a cop?" it asked.

Twitchell ticked his head at Burnley. "Take this young fellow down to the Bail Plaza to settle his fine." Smiling at Burnley, Twitchell said, "He'll get you there faster than the public transit. Right, O'Brien?"

"That I will." O'Brien grabbed Burnley and hustled him out into the street.

The black Police Service cruiser was skimming through the night sky. Burnley glanced down at the pocked floor to see what was rattling. He dropped to his knees. One of the large jointed sections of the floor was loose and flapping. Burnley waited a few seconds in the empty compartment and then tugged up the flap. No alarms sounded. Just below he saw tower tops. This was near the famed old Mexican section of the Greater Los Angeles and the penthouses were all adobe and thatch. When the cruiser was gliding a few feet above a transplanted mission Burnley shoved himself out and into the night.

He made a ragged half cartwheel and landed on dusty red tiles. He slid with a slaty grating sound off the mission souvenir shop roof and landed against the praying Indians tableau. While he lay flat and still and listened to the cruiser fade away Burnley tried to determine whether he'd broken anything without actually moving. He seemed okay.

A mechanical swallow hopped onto the small of his back and pecked. No one else seemed around. Burnley got to his knees, whacked the bird away, and moved through the darkness to the edge of the building. There was a regulation firepole attached to the building side. He rested his elbows on the adobe wall and then swung out. The police cruiser still hadn't missed him. With luck he'd get to the street and out of sight before there was any alarm.

There was a possibility that they were deliberately trying to keep him from Francesca. Be that as it may, Burnley was bent on seeing the girl. He needed no advice now.

By the time Burnley gained access to Francesca's apartment building again, a full three days later, she had moved. Avoiding the police and devising an entry ruse had taken much longer than he'd counted on. Three separate people had required bribing and two androids dismantling to bring it off.

Francesca had left no forwarding address. Burnley was not stopped. He carried the image of her, willowy and redheaded, always with him. He knew some kind of lover's homing instinct would guide him to her.

The tempo of the quest slowed, however. As a fugitive from the police he could no longer work for the Welfare Bureau. Boke Fonseca, his Immediate Chief, had been sympathetic when Burnley had risked a call to him. It was due to Fonseca that Burnley had food to go on, three dozen cartons of Rice Surprise. Burnley found lodgings in one of the Skid Row sectors. The better Skid Row was full up and wouldn't even put his alias on a waiting list. He was finally able to get a piece of floor space in a Skid Row suburb that didn't even get handout aid.

He was able to keep himself looking presentable enough to scout Sector 28 and try to locate Francesca at her place of work. After five days of reconnoitering he learned that she had been transferred to a girly book throwaway firm in the San Diego area of Greater LA.

With his remaining rice and money Burnley set off to the south. An unemployed jingle machine operator who'd had the floor space three squares over from him had told Burnley there was still something of the old Pacific Coast Highway intact. It was seldom policed and, therefore, a good bet for drifters aiming for Mexico.

The Shanghai Commission got Burnley before he was much beyond the Laguna Beach sector. Not one of the andys tumbled to the fact that he was a fugitive. They accepted his alias. As a drifter he could be conscripted by SC.

A week later, waking from a dream of Francesca and the cool sharp scent of her, Burnley found himself on a cruise ship that ran excursions between Mars and Venus. His job, he learned, was to keep the piped music systems in order. Out here there was none of the smooth efficient automatic music of Greater Los Angeles. Burnley put in long cramped days cranking turntables, goosing disc changers and nudging tape spools.

It was on the morning that he realized he had been separated from Francesca for a longer period than he had originally spent with her that Burnley led the mutiny. It was a thick warm day in a repair port near Venusburg. Burnley and six men overpowered the captain and flew the ship off toward the British Territories of Mars. Inspired by his need to see Francesca, Burnley was a very compelling leader.

He even moved two androids into joining his cause.

The landing on Mars was mismanaged and the ship crashed roughly one hundred kilometers from the nearest British colony. Sand storms and a flurry of cannibalism cut down the survivors and three weeks after the crash Burnley and an android named Gruber were alone on a vast rambling red-swarded plain. Gruber shorted-out in some obscure way and took to speaking of nothing but the capitals of states. Burnley had enjoyed discussing Francesca with Gruber but he dismantled him now and continued on alone.

Nearly a month later, at a run-down Public Oasis that the British had built and then abandoned, Burnley was sure he saw Francesca. Her enigmatic smile, her red hair flickering in the hot wind, her rangy walk. The desert raiders who captured him at this point assured him it was a mirage. Burnley would not debate the subject.

The raiders were made up of some three hundred native Martians and nine British remittance men. The leader, a leathery off-green man, never tired of kidding Burnley about his mirage. One dry dusty afternoon Burnley got the man's knife away from him and killed him. This automatically promoted him to the position of leader.

Burnley developed a knack for planning. He decided that if he could take over the nearest British settlement, Fort Huxley, he would be in a strong bargaining position. He could then ask to be taken back to Greater Los Angeles on Earth. Of course England would have to arrange for dismissal of his loitering charge.

The fall of Fort Huxley to Burnley's raiders set off a large slave revolt among rival raiders and caused Britain to send additional troops to Mars. A successful merger arranged by Burnley put him in charge of nearly eight thousand fighting men of the desert. He realized now that he would have to take over this whole section of Mars in order to get Britain to listen to him. So far they would not bargain. He proceeded.

The wind struck at the tent and swirled waves of sand under the edges. Burnley's maps were gritty. He dropped onto his favorite folding chair and frowned. He loosened his robe and unbuckled his holster. He put the blaster pistol and his best knife on top of a small table and hunched back, closing his eyes.

"At last," said a parched voice.

Burnley opened his eyes. "What?"

A thin sun-spotted man in a sand-tattered Earth suit came hopping into the tent, arms flapping. Two raiders followed, picked the small man up and gave him another toss. The man hopped and flapped almost to Burnley's chair.

"Who is this?" asked Burnley.

"He has a diplomatic pass," said one of the guards. "More than likely a spy. We brought him to you."

"I'm from Greater Los Angeles," said the man. "From the Government Lovelorn Bureau."

Burnley straightened. "Leave me with this man."

"It's taken me several long uncomfortable weeks to track you down. My name is Borman."

"You said the Lovelorn Bureau?"

Borman sighed. "Yes. And do I feel embarrassed. I don't know if you know it or not but behind the precise and mechanized smoothness of the Lovelorn Bureau there is a large human staff."

"I didn't know that."

"Well," said Borman. "What can I say? Once in a long while one of those silly machines errs."

Borman cleared his throat. "Excuse me. This desert wind tires me out. I don't know how you put up with it," he rasped hoarsely.

"I've been here two years."

"Yes." Borman sighed again. "All a mistake. The Decision Wing caught it at the last Annual Review Session. You see, Francesca Anders is the girl for you. You are the boy for her. Admittedly she had a slight restlessness problem. Simple shock therapy from one of our mobile units fixed that up. She's now fit as a fiddle and waiting for you."

"What are you telling me?"

"That we made a mistake," said Borman. "Our machines did. That's the trouble with machines. Which is why we have a special fund to track down and rectify mistakes. Yours has been one of my most challenging cases. You've cut quite a swath. Fortunately it is over at last, Mr. Burnley. You can come back to Greater Los Angeles and marry Francesca."

"Look," said Burnley. "I make my own decisions now. Nobody, real or machine, gives me orders."

Borman frowned. "You love her?"

"Nobody tells me who to love."

"I'm afraid," said Borman, sighing once more, "I'm much too late."

"Meaning?"

"You seem to have what I like to call grail seekers' trouble."

"Don't get allegorical."

"I mean," said Borman, "that you've been at this too long. The object of your quest is no longer important. The quest itself has become everything."

Burnley's eyes narrowed. "Those," he said, reaching down for his knife, "are fighting words."

7

The Katy Dialogues

Katy Priestly hadn't made a flic in ten years, but they didn't know that out here on Panam. The public relations fac-robot would still stir up a lot of interest for the latest showing of *Earth Is Earth, Mars Is Mars* in the stereo houses. They still had TV on Panam. The PR robot would come over great on a vague medium like that. The few slight dents wouldn't show at all.

Larson in the Jupiter office, where Ben Hollis had picked the equipment up, said the gimmick had gone over big there. Ben was sure it would work here on Panam. And, of course, so was everybody at the Biz Enterprises office in the capital.

The BE ship was sailing in toward the capital port, about five thousand feet up, when it started to wobble wildly. Ben Hollis reached out for the *Emergency Manual*, knocking over three bound volumes of *Mars Variety*, but by the time he'd come to *wobble* in the index the small ship was drifting in gentle zigzags down and down. And when he'd turned to page 481 the ship slammed into the ground, everything rattled and Ben blacked out. He never had been too good with mechanical things.

When he determined that he was alive and that the radio was working Ben sent in a report to the Biz Enterprises office. He was responsible for getting the Katy Priestly robot and the open-end spools to the capital in time for the big premiere. It was his first solo public relations job since he'd been transferred to Panam from Venus. This position was a lot more interesting and a lot more fun than selling LP's to the natives on Venus. Biz Enterprises had faith in him or they wouldn't have promoted him. He had to prove himself.

Ottkins answered his call. "No time for much chat, Ben. Where are you location-wise?"

"I had a little bad luck, Ott. I seem to have crashed. I think I'm in a valley out here. But the robot's fine."

"Just sit tight. Did you take a reading with your tridiviner?"

"I think it's broke."

"Well, we'll come and find you as soon as we get back." "Back?"

"Everybody here's off for sort of a holiday."

"But, Ott, I got the stuff for the premiere."

"Premiere's postponed, guy. See, the natives have sort of gone amok here on Panam. You know how hard it is to deal with folks when they're excited. They already roasted the gang at the Coke Embassy. We're closing up shop till tempers cool."

"Yeah, but, Ott, I'm lost out here."

"No worry at all, Ben. This will blow over in a few weeks and we'll come out and find you. You've got your emergency kit. Just take a little vacation on us. And keep your eye on that robot. You're a good man, Ben. Hey, they're trying to slice up Thompson with those little knives of theirs. Got to get on that and stop it. See you. Good luck."

The radio wouldn't talk to him after that. But even if he was lost Ben Hollis had his assignment.

Ben looked in on the Katy Priestly robot twice a day during his first week in the valley. He lived on the rations in his emergency kit and studied his *Emergency Manual*. He explored the valley, which was hot and semi-tropical and seemed to have no obvious exits. At night he would read *Mars Variety*, drink a cup of emergency cocoa and turn in. Nobody came to rescue him.

The BE *Manual* was a really fine book. It taught Ben Hollis which growing things were edible and which were poisonous. It taught him how to set traps and what to do with the animals he caught.

Before he'd been in LP Sales Ben had worked on a monitor squad and one of the shows he'd watched regularly was a Venusian cooking class. About his third week in the valley he fixed all his meals Venusian style. An hour or two a day he'd sit by the radio, but nobody called. He'd never been able to contact the capital after the first day. But he was still on assignment. So he looked after the PR robot and waited.

From the BE *Manual Supplement* he learned how to build a hut. When he got that finished he moved most of his equipment in there. The crate with Katy Priestly, too, because he was still keeping an eye on that. When the premiere did come off, the robot would have to be ship-shape.

You can't take Venusian cooking all the time. Ben switched to Martian recipes the fourth week. The rainy cycle was starting on Panam and trapping was getting more complex. Ben featured more dishes with fruit and vegetables.

One wet, gray afternoon Ben built a fire in his hand-wrought stone fireplace, following advice he'd found in a letter to the editor of the BE *Manual Annual*. The rain was falling heavily on the roof, which he'd never been able to get completely weatherproof.

Ben was worried about the Katy Priestly robot. He wasn't an expert mechanic, but he had the idea the robot might rust or something. Following the instructions on the crate he unpacked the robot and set it in the chair he'd made out of yap bark. Katy Priestly was, when she made her films anyway, a slim girl with light blond hair and a medium tan. She had a dent on her forehead, but that didn't detract any. Larson had told Ben that at the height of Katy's career there had been twenty-five of these robots in circulation doing public relations and publicity for her pictures.

After reading the directions carefully through twice Ben found the slot in the back of the robot's neck, under the hair where it didn't show, and inserted the first of the open-end tapes. He decided to give the robot a test run to see if it was still in tiptop condition.

Going through the excelsior in the bottom of the crate Ben found the booklet with the interviewer's questions in it. Beside each question was the time the interviewer had to ask it and beside the answers the time of each response.

Ben had taken the BE night school course in Showman-ship and he figured he could run through the questions well enough for a test. He looked them over and clicked on Katy Priestly.

"Well, how do you like it here on Panam, Miss Priestly?" Ben asked the warming-up robot without even a hesitation at the spot where you had to fill in the planet name.

"Why, I think it's wonderful being here. I've always wanted to visit," answered the robot. Her voice was low, but with a young-girl quality to it.

"Your latest picture is called *Earth Is Earth, Mars Is Mars*. What sort of a picture is it?"

"It's all about love. The funny things it does to you. The way a sensitive young girl feels, you know," she said. There was no sign of rust.

"This is your fifth picture. Right, Miss Priestly?"

"That's right. And I've enjoyed them all."

Ben ran through the questions and the robot responded convincingly each time. It was a believable tape, with a relaxed message that came across well. After getting Katy Priestly's advice to young actors Ben said, "Thank you for dropping by, Miss Priestly," and clicked off the robot.

BE would be glad to know the situation. Ben slipped on his rainslicker and ran across the high yellow grass to the ship. There was still no reply at BE headquarters. He sat listening to the rain on the ship's hull for several minutes and then ran back to his hut and the fire.

If he hadn't been on assignment Ben Hollis would have worried more than he did. He knew BE would come for him as soon as they could. Meanwhile he had the Katy robot to take care of.

As the rainy season progressed Ben spent more time in the hut. By rereading the BE *Manual* he'd been able to fix the roof so that there was only one minor leak in the far corner.

For the sake of efficiency, to routinize his assignment, Ben established the procedure of checking out Katy each morning. He would run through both open-end tapes, watching carefully for any signs of mechanical breakdown. It wasn't surprising, considering his grades in Showmanship, that he memorized the questions quickly and didn't have to consult the script.

Mornings were always enjoyable because of his work. Some of the long afternoons, with rain falling heavy all around, unsettled him. Not much, but a little.

Once each afternoon Ben would get into his rain gear and make a dash for the ship. He would warm up the radio and try to contact the capital. The most he ever got was a dry squawking sound.

He learned from the Orientation Section of the BE *Manual* that the rain would be letting up soon. In the last of the dark, rainy afternoons he set up the practice of giving Katy a second check. He ran through the tapes and noted his reactions to them, noted how the machine seemed to be operating. This meant more paperwork, but Ben felt it was better to be safe than sorry.

Ben was stretched out in the dry yellow grass, his eyes half closed, when the idea occurred to him. With the rains passed it was pleasant in the valley. And he had his job to keep him occupied during the day. Still he missed, not all the time but now and then, people and conversation. He checked three times a day now, but the questions had become automatic to him and it hardly seemed like real conversation anymore.

However, though Katy's responses were set, it occurred to him that there was no reason why he couldn't vary his questions. Not during office hours. Probably in the evening. Evenings were warm now and he kept the hut door open.

After dinner, back in Venusian style this week, Ben slipped a tape into Katy's neck and clicked her on. Timing was going to be the problem. . . .

"Well, we've been in this valley two months huh, Katy? Getting bored?" he asked, feeling a little silly.

"I think it's wonderful being here. I've always wanted to visit," she said, a hint of a smile in her voice.

"Still, you've looked worried lately. What's bothering you?"

"It's all about love. The funny things it does to you. The way a sensitive young girl feels, you know."

"You love me? Kate, all these months you have?"

"That's right. And I've enjoyed them all."

Ben laughed here and got behind. He had to rush the next questions.

He decided to end on a serious note. "You do think things will work out here, don't you, Katy?"

"Yes. You've got to stick with it. Hard work is the key to success. And sticking to it. You've got to have patience. That's my advice," Katy said with conviction.

"Well, thank you, Katy."

"Thank you."

Twice during the night Ben woke up and found himself laughing.

During the pollen-drift season Ben discovered he had an allergy. He stayed in more, going out only for food and his visit to the ship radio.

He worked only half a day now and spent the afternoons reading up on sneezing and coughing in the *Manual*. Sometimes he would read sections of *Mars Variety* aloud to Katy. Sometimes he would just have a chat with her. Using both tapes and flicking the switch off and on Ben could talk up to an hour without any repetition from Katy. Tape 2 was mostly details about Katy's early life and ambitions. That got Ben to talking about his own childhood.

"I grew up on Mars," Ben said one afternoon. "With my uncle and aunt. How about you, Katy?"

"I was born in St. Paul, Minnesota, U.S.A. On Earth, you know," Katy said.

"My dad was from Madison, Wisconsin. He was an art director for Earth & Associates, PR Division. He died when I was six. Maybe we could visit Earth sometime."

"Earth. Yes. You're always loyal to your home planet. Of course, I love your planet, too."

"And you like me. I'm glad."

"You should be."

Toward evening Ben started pacing the stone floor he'd

made for the hut. He began talking to Katy. Finally he asked her, "Katy, do you really think they'll come for us? Maybe we should try to get out of here and go look for them. Or do you think we should stay?"

"Yes. You've got to stick with it. Hard work is the key to success. And sticking to it. You've got to have patience. That's my advice," she said.

"Yeah, I guess you're right."

"Thank you."

Ben sat down on the floor and watched the empty fireplace. "Good old Katy," he said.

Ben came back from the ship and got out of his jacket across the room from Katy. "Another dust storm," he said. "Dust-storm season is starting." He shook the coat out carefully and came and stood in front of Katy. "I still can't make contact with BE. I don't know."

"Why, I think it's wonderful being here. I've always wanted to visit."

"Doesn't it get you? Why are you cheerful, Katy?"

"It's all about love," she said, her voice soft. "The funny things it does to you. The way a sensitive young girl feels, you know."

"Well, maybe it's love. Christ, though it seems like we've been here for years."

"That's right. And I've enjoyed them all."

Ben changed the subject. He might as well just talk small talk with Katy. But finally he had to say, "But my God, Katy, why have they just left us here for months? I like BE. Don't they like me? Look, let's leave here. Try to go to them. Maybe they've forgotten. They have lots of things on their minds." He looked into her face. "Katy? You don't still think we should wait? Huh?"

"Yes. You've got to stick with it. Hard work is the key to success. And sticking to it. You've got to have patience."

"You really believe that?"

"That's my advice."

"I suppose. I suppose BE will come. Sure, Katy, you're right."

"Thank you."

The rain hit soft on the roof, drops falling slow. Ben tossed a dry log into his fireplace and turned to Katy. "I had good ratings on all my tests. A little low in mechanical skills. But good in sales logic. And people relations. I mean, BE wouldn't just abandon me without looking."

"Love makes the universe go round," Katy said, smiling.

"You're being smart now. I suppose it's your privilege. You're a famous actress and all."

"Just a simple Earth girl," Katy said.

"Sure. But, really, Katy, I've done my job all this time. By now I should even be in line for a raise. I've looked after you and kept records. I'm sure BE will take that into consideration."

"Yes, it's a wonderful emotional experience."

"What is? Us being here?" He took her by the shoulder. "You still want us to stay? You think BE is going to come?"

"Yes. You've got to stick with it. Hard work is the key to success. And sticking to it. You've got to have patience."

Holding both Katy's shoulders Ben said, "Good God, Katy, we've known each other for months. We know all about each other. Can't you understand me? You see how I feel, don't you?"

"Thank you." Katy smiled.

Ben stepped back from her. "You don't really at all. All you give me is public relations crap for BE." His foot swung out and slammed into Katy's stomach. "Well, screw them."

Katy clanged over onto the floor, huddling her limbs together. Ben kicked her again and kept kicking her until her head rolled off and into the corner by the fireplace, trailing tubes and wires.

"I'm knocking off work," he said.

He went to the ship to tell BE about it. But they wouldn't answer. He kicked in the radio, too.

The rain came down fast. Ben stood in the grass and looked up into the sky. The rain fell harder and harder on his face. That was good. He was crying, but it would never show.

Anybody who followed the BE *Manual* knew you should wear your rainslicker when out in the rain. "Screw them," Ben said. He'd come out without his coat.

Ben sat in the sun on the porch of his hut with his mouth tightly closed. One of these days he'd gather Katy up. Not that it would do any good. He'd never be able to fix her. He had a low mechanical skills rating.

He was really sorry about Katy. To punish himself he refused to talk to anybody.

Now that the sun had come back that was hard. All the animals had come back, too. They had started talking to him and not knowing his reasons for keeping quiet they might be offended. It was bad public relations, but it couldn't be helped.

Same went for the trees and the rocks. He wasn't talking, he was punishing himself.

And that went for the flowers, too. Not a word. Although sometimes their funny squeaky voices made him laugh out loud.

8

Nobody Starves

The straight falling rain blurred the glass wall of the cubicle and Arlen Lembeck could not see any of the billboards that dotted this sector of Greater Los Angeles. Or maybe it was his eyesight. He'd been docked one hundred calories for missing punch-in last Tuesday and he had the feeling his new eating program was affecting his vision. He leaned back in his chair until the headrest was a half inch from the headrest of his cubicle chief and picked up the ear trumpet that fed into Secretary Central.

The quota of subliminal outdoor billboard slogans for Cubicle 97 of the Greater Los Angeles Subliminal Outdoor Bureau was twenty-five this week. Going over quota could mean ten more calories a day and a membership card in one of the new Venusian import warehouses. Lembeck didn't understand Venusian imports but Edith was still upset about the calorie cut and something like this might boost her feelings.

Though he was thirty-four and only a Class B14 Lembeck was a good slogan man. The *Cubicles 90–100 News-letter* had mentioned him twice in the last month.

"Touching," said Burns Smollet, the cubicle chief.

"Sorry," said Lembeck. Accidentally his chair had ticked against his chief's.

Smollet was only a week past his thirty-first birthday. He was a B10 and had been for six months. Of course he'd been given credit for his Propaganda Corps Reserve time. Edith was not up on protocol and Smollet's age and rank bothered her. Smollet was a pretty fair slogan man, though.

A small pink card slapped out of the In slot and landed face down next to Lembeck's left hand. Absently, like a confident card player, Lembeck turned the punch card over. "Report 8:45 tomorrow (the 25th) for Termination Processing," it read. "Wing 6 of the Pre-Termination Board, Hollywood & Vine, Greater Los Angeles, Sector 28. Thank you for the interest you've shown."

Lembeck swallowed. "They can't fire me on a Wednesday," he said.

"There was a memo to that effect last month," said Smollet. "Are they?"

Lembeck held up the pink card. "I have to turn in all my cards, food and everything, and go back to the Employment Complex." He had been with the Outdoor Bureau for seven years, since before his marriage.

"No sweat," said Smollet. "They'll fix you up in no time. And after all, these days, nobody starves."

That was a nice slogan. "Thanks for reminding me," said Lembeck. "You're right."

"Now that that's settled," said Smollet, "let's get going on the quota. I'm going to have a hell of a time breaking in a new man and not slowing the stride of Cubicle 97."

The other two men in the cubicle looked up and nodded sympathetically at Lembeck. Then everybody got going on the slogans.

The Pre-Termination Board was fully automated so it wasn't as embarrassing as it might have been. The last time Lembeck had been here, seven years ago, they'd had fac-human androids. Now everything looked like a machine. Except the doorman who, in keeping with an old robotics tradition, was made in the image of a Negro.

Waiting in the Card Surrendering Room Foyer Lembeck let himself loosen up a little. He stretched his legs and made fists of his hands a few times. Edith had taken it all pretty well. The Power Bureau had jumped the gun and cut everything off but Edith had rounded up some candles and they'd had a pretty romantic dinner. The pantry outlet had scrambled at midnight and nothing would come out but garbage so they'd skipped their midnight wafers. Edith was confident that the Employment Complex would do something nice for him this time.

Holding hands in the candle-lit dining cubicle they'd even suggested to each other that someone had had Lembeck fired so that he could be switched to a better job. It did seem a possibility.

Edith had not had an Employment Card since four years ago when the clinical android at her office had decided she was pregnant. Their live doctor had disagreed but by that time the card was cancelled and the waiting list for married women in Edith's age and rank group was closed until such a time as conditions shifted. That was all right. Lembeck had never had a bad deal from the Employment Complex.

Things got disturbing over on Sunset in the Post-Termination Board offices. The big Temporary Food Card machine was making an odd whirring sound. Finally it said, "Lembeck, Lembeck, Arlen, Arlen."

"Yes, sir?" Lembeck said, watching the bright grey machine. It was ten feet high and ten feet wide and, as he watched, the little brass plate with the manufacturer's name popped off and the four little zuber screws pinged on the imitation floor.

"Lembeck, Lembeck, Lembeck, Arlen, Arlen, Arlen," said the Food Card machine.

"Yes, I'm right here. I was told to check with you people before I went over to the Employment Complex. So that I could have a Temporary Food Card until I am put through Pre-Indoctrination by my new place of employment. And then I have to get all my other cards here, too, and see somebody about getting my parking receipt validated."

"Lemlen Arbeck Becklem Lenlem Beckbeck Lenlen Ararar," said the machine.

"Arlen Lembeck," corrected Lembeck.

Two more zuber screws popped out from unseen place. "Follow the red line and your processing will continue."

A throbbing scarlet line, six inches wide, appeared on the floor and snaked like down hill water for a door in the far wall. Once through it Lembeck found himself outside on Sunset Boulevard.

"It'll be okay," he told himself. He put his timevox to his ear and it told him it was sixteen minutes from his appointment at the Employment Complex. And that was way down on Spring Street in Sector 54. He would have to come back to Post-Termination later. He reminded himself to ask somebody at Employment Complex about it.

It was the first time he'd seen an android cry. This one was in Re-Placement and looked something like an A10 with extra calorie allotments. Lembeck asked, "Nothing?"

"Look," said the android, holding a sheaf of graphs up to Lembeck. It sniffed quietly. "Though less than human, Mr. Lembeck, I pride myself on having more than a human share of compassion." Its wide unwrinkled head shook from side to side, deflecting the course of the tears. "Your aptitude tests are depressing."

"Couldn't I take new tests? After all, those were done seven years ago when I was still a young man in my 20s."

"No, no," said the android, smoothing the graphs out on the desk. "These were made just today."

"When? I've only been here twelve minutes."

"That revolving door you came through is no ordinary revolving door." The android nodded. "Take my word for it, Mr. Lembeck, if there's one thing we know about you with a certainty it's your aptitudes."

"There must be something."

"You see," said the android, "the demand for ceramics is so small at present. Most authorities seem to agree that the Venusian imports are ceramic in nature. The balance of import and local products and the surplus storage factors involved in the output of Greater Los Angeles make chances pretty slim for anyone in the ceramics line."

"But I'm a slogan writer. I was a B14 in Subliminal Outdoor," said Lembeck. "I'm not a ceramicist. My job classification card will show that."

"The cards in your case are still processing over in Sector 28," said the android. "Besides the aptitude figures show that you're a ceramicist. You may feel some inclinations in other directions, but we can't honestly put you into a new job where you'll be unhappy and frustrated."

"I was happy for seven years as a slogan writer."

"As you say, though, you entered that line at an early unformed age. Now, wiser and more mature, your real strengths and weaknesses shine through. You can be sure we'll keep you on file. Venusian imports may be only a fad."

"Isn't there some temporary job?"

"You wouldn't be happy in an uncertain situation like that."

"Well," said Lembeck, "there's a problem in that I didn't get any temporary food cards and lodging cards and all the rest of the cards when I was at Post-Termination. Something went wrong and then it was late and I had to rush over here. I even had to pay for my own parking."

"I don't believe," said the android, "that anything can have gone wrong. If you wish to make another appointment to see Post-Termination I can get you the forms to fill out."

"Fine. Could I get another appointment today?"

"You can't even get the forms until next week."

"And the new job?"

"Possibly toward the spring if current trends remain constant."

"What do my wife and I do till then? See, we don't have any food cards at all. She doesn't work at present and I had to surrender all my cards at Pre-Termination. So if . . ."

"Mr. Lembeck," interrupted the android, "let me assure you. Nobody starves. I would suggest, considering the personal nature of your problem, that you consult the Therapy Wing over at Welfare Hub. They're out by the beach over in Sector 24. It's a pleasant drive out there since the rain's let up."

"Thanks," said Lembeck, standing up.

"Would you mind leaving by the side door? If you go back through the revolving door that'll produce another aptitude test. One more like this will depress me even more."

Lembeck used the side door.

Therapy was closed for alterations and the Information Booth in the Welfare Hub's Alternate Lobby suggested that Lembeck try the Motor Club of Southern California.

"The Motor Club?"

"Oops, oops," said the booth. "Sorry, Mr. Lembeck. Correcting. With your problem you had best see the Abraham Lincoln, Etc. Handout Kitchen in Sector 54, down on Central Street. They'll give you a food bundle and a good word until you get on your feet again."

"Thank you."

"No trouble. They have lots of road maps."

All the androids at the Abraham Lincoln, Etc. Handout Kitchen had beards. According to a sign in the Waiting Room today's special was veal wafers.

"Welcome, son," said a whiskered android. "In the name of Abraham Lincoln, Theodore Roosevelt, Warren Gamaliel Harding, Barry Goldwater and 17 Latter Day Great Americans let me welcome you." He handed Lembeck a 9 by 12 punch hole sheet of blue paper and a pen, which was chained to his wrist. "Sign that and your package of nourishing food will be handed to you with the sincere best wishes of a group of citizens who, although they are too proud to let themselves sink down to poverty and too energetic not to rise to A rank, nevertheless take pity on those unfortunates who are lazy and indigent and have a natural sense of rhythm in many cases and just don't want to work for their bread or, as is the case today, veal wafers."

Lembeck read the paper over. "This says I swear under threat of criminal prosecution that I have never cadged a meal from the Abraham Lincoln, Etc. Handout Kitchen before and won't ever come whining back here again."

"It's our way of teaching you to do and dare, risk and rise, stand and deliver," said the android. "Sign by the little x's."

Lembeck hadn't eaten since the night before and it was now nearly dusk. He signed.

Two days later Lembeck had to divorce his wife. He and Edith still loved each other. In fact, the candlelight suppers had brought them closer together. But the Real Estate Council had evicted them from their two-room apartment on the twenty-sixth floor of the Zanuck-Sahara Building and before Edith could move back in with her mother she had to be legally divorced from Lembeck. Living with her mother seemed to be the only way to get immediate food for Edith. The Abraham Lincoln, Etc. Handout Kitchen must have circulated Lembeck's name on their daily ne'er-do-well lists. When he went to a Food Dole Shelter two IBM machines blacked his eye and tossed him out. The Post-Termination Board gave him an appointment a month hence for a pre-interview to reconsider his request for a

Temporary Food Card. The only thing that had come off smoothly and quickly was the divorce.

After that Edith was able to sneak food to Lembeck once a day. Her mother, though, was on a Pensioner's Low Calorie Food Allotment and even with an Incompetent Dependent Food Card in the offing for Edith there wasn't much chance of a lot of food coming out of the pantry outlet at Edith's mother's.

From an unemployed TV novelist, with whom he had been ejected from a Down-But-Not-Out One Night Sleep Hostel, Lembeck learned that the Adopt A Misfit Center might help him.

"You mean I can get a job with them?"

"No," said the ex-TV novelist, guiding Lembeck into a thin slit of an alley that was policed by an android cop with a defective tube that made him night blind. "Here. We can sleep here tonight."

"I've been sleeping in my car," said Lembeck, settling down on some weeds, "but the Greater Los Angeles Credit Authority took it back a couple days ago. Because I missed my regular $38.01 payment. If I'd had my savings account I could have done something. It turns out I forgot to send in my monthly statements saying that I wasn't planning to withdraw the money. They've been taking out a service charge of $8 and so the savings are gone."

"You're going to be perfect for the Adopt A Misfit Center."

"But not for a job?"

"No. Childless couples go there to adopt whatever they want. Not everyone wants a troublesome little kid. There are those who prefer maturity. When I was on top I adopted six 50-year-old men just to bounce my ideas off of. Those days we had the big six-room place in the Benedict Canyon sector of Greater LA."

"Somebody would want to adopt a 34-year-old ex-slogan writer?"

"Maybe," said the ex-novelist, leaning back against the slick wall of the building. "Me they didn't want. Ex-TV novelists depress people."

"I'll make an appointment," said Lembeck.

That night he dreamed of wafers.

The day before Lembeck visited the Adopt A Misfit Center an A2 couple from the Palm Springs sector of Greater Los Angeles had come in and adopted a 43-year-old ceramicist. That meant there would be a thirty-day waiting period before Lembeck's application could be considered. The lobby of the Misfit Center did give him a cup of near-coffee and two donut wafers and that took care of the food problem for another day. That was Tuesday.

On Wednesday Lembeck got by on the food Edith slipped him. Thursday an A5 dropped a twenty-calorie coupon in Lembeck's hand in front of a Martian-style foodamat and Lembeck went in and had twenty calories worth of something thick and light blue. He now weighed fifteen pounds less than his usual one hundred fifty and his beard had filled out. The rest of the week he tried making the rounds of Termination Boards and welfare outlets again in hope of getting an earlier appointment. All he got was a small red punchcard listing him as a Chronic Malcontent. He had to carry the card with him at all times or pay a fine.

On Sunday Lembeck found the All-Purpose Automatic Religious Center. It had never occurred to him to turn to the church for help but as he was walking by the bright silver building in the derelict sector of Greater Los Angeles a strong aroma of hot soup drifted out over the gold turnstiles and Lembeck was compelled to go inside.

There were, surprisingly, considering the strong food scents inside, only two other people in the great vaulted room. An old C-rating derelict in frayed gray sports clothes and an attractive blonde girl of about twenty. The girl had on a clean pair of faded denim pants and a pale tartan shirt.

The sniffling C-rating derelict was sitting in front of the Buddhist display and the girl knelt before an automatic religious android whose denomination Lembeck couldn't place.

The smell of soup, and possibly a meat course, was strong in the big shadow-ceilinged room. Lembeck couldn't locate its source. He picked a friendly-looking scarlet-robed android and pushed the On button.

"What is life without a purpose, without a goal," said the android in a warm rich voice.

"Could you tell me where the dining room is?"

"What is life without a goal? I will tell you, my son. A hollow shell."

"I didn't eat yesterday. I thought, noticing the aroma, that I might be able to arrange for a meal here."

"Those of us who have fallen from the main currents of Greater Los Angeles Society need goals, too. And though it is truly said that nobody starves in this day and age, nevertheless a certain hunger can grow up."

"That's right," agreed Lembeck.

"A two-year hitch with the Martian Reclamation And Roadway Corps provides you with a goal, a purpose and three minimum calorie requirement meals each and every day," said the android. "When I have finished my sermon an application blank will issue from the slot marked goal. Sign it and put it back in the slot. This time tomorrow you will be enroute to the red planet on a fine ship where meals of great warmth and nourishment are served at regular hours. Sign, my son."

"I don't want to go to Mars. I have an ex-wife down by the ocean. I just want something to eat until I get a job."

"Life is nice when you have a purpose," said the android and clicked off.

An application form dropped out into Lembeck's hand.

"Don't," said a voice at his side.

It was the blonde girl. "Ma'am?"

"The other guy's too far gone for us but you might do. Want to join?"

"Join what?"

"Tell you outside," she said. "Come on."

"I don't want to go to Mars."

"Neither do we."

"Couldn't I see somebody about a bowl of soup?"

"There's no food here."

"The smell."

"It's a chemical substance they feed into blowers," she said, nodding her head at the ceiling.

Lembeck went outside with the girl.

Sawtelle was a tall grizzle-whiskered man, thin in his khaki coat and pants. He handed Lembeck a half a vegetable wafer and a real piece of near-cheese. The food caught a pleasant glow from the campfire. "I have a hundred in my group so far," Sawtelle said. "Dotted all over the Sierra Madres here." He pointed at the hundred million lights of Greater Los Angeles fanning away far below. "Misfits and unemployables. We don't eat well. But we do, with our raids and our experimental gardens, manage to eat without taking charity."

The blonde girl, her name was Margery McCracklin, was one of Sawtelle's recruiters. She was sitting quietly across the cave.

Lembeck, watching her as he ate, noticed that her wrists were narrow and sharp, her ankles, too. It had taken them a long time to climb up here into the mountains to Sawtelle's temporary encampment. "You steal food and supplies?" Lembeck asked. He broke the piece of cheese into four sections, making each one last four bites.

"Yes," said Sawtelle. "Only from the A class and the top half of the Bs. Those who have well above the minimum."

"I have an ex-wife," said Lembeck. "If I joined you would I be able to see her?"

"I have an ex-wife, too," said Sawtelle. "Margery has an ex-child. We all try to pay visits and give over what food we can."

Lembeck ran his tongue over his teeth. "I hate to hurt my job chances."

Margery laughed. "You'll probably never get called back in. Once you get edged out of the system you seldom get back."

"It has nothing to do with you," said Sawtelle. "With an almost 100% automatic employment and welfare system in Greater Los Angeles little kinks are bound to show up now and then."

"I'll never work again?"

"That's what," said Margery, hunching toward the small fire, "has happened to most of us. If you get another chance with them they need never know about this part of your life."

"They usually only check for an actual conviction record," said Sawtelle. "You could be given a criminal inclinations aptitude test. You could get caught." He cut himself a hunk of near-cheese from the piece in his jacket pocket.

"All right," said Lembeck. "What the hell. Okay."

Margery smiled at him.

An A class housewife in a four-room ranch-style house in the Pasadena sector of Greater Los Angeles shot Margery dead on the third food raid Lembeck went on.

Lembeck kept running, a package of turkey wafers under his coat. There was no doubt that Margery was gone. The blaster pistol had lit up the night long enough for him to see her die over his shoulder.

At dawn he was well into the mountains. But where Sawtelle was he had no idea. Margery had been his partner on all his missions and, since Lembeck was still breaking in, Margery had been entrusted with the pattern of campsite shifts.

Day came on and Lembeck opened the package of wafers and ate two, chewing and swallowing fast as he climbed. His stomach made unsettled sounds and he stopped finally and ate a whole handful of the turkey wafers.

The brush was thick and there were clusters of trees up here. Lembeck had trouble breathing and he knew that he must have climbed higher than he had realized. He made it over a rise and found a narrow path leading down into a slight cuplike clearing. This would be a good place to rest.

He sat on a mossy rock and ate another handful of wafers and then the box was empty. Lembeck dropped it between his feet. That was wrong. He decided to hide the empty box.

Off to his right a thick growth of thorny bushes tangled together over a crevice. He went over to stuff the empty wafer carton in there. His hand and arm got scratched as he slid the box in through the thorns. He cocked his wrist to fling the box away. But the box hit against something solid. Lembeck shoved both hands in and forced the bushes aside. He saw now a door handle.

"Well, let's see now," he said. He twisted one arm up to guard his face and head and then pushed around the bushes. He caught the handle and turned it. A door opened in and he fell forward and onto a slanting corridor. His hand still on the handle he looked at the door. A small plate on it read: "Nuclear Emergency Food Storehouse No. Twenty. Stocked by the Pasadena Chamber of Commerce, May, 1991."

Lembeck left the door open and moved down the corridor. When he hit the end of the incline lights went on in the room beyond. "It's stayed in working order all these years," he said.

The room was bigger than the apartment he and Edith had had and it seemed to be surrounded by other rooms. On shelves on two walls there were packages of preserved foods and in the room's center there was something labeled Safe Water Well. Another room had smoked meats, the real stuff, and bottles of wine and brandy and whiskey. There were packages and containers of foods Lembeck had only heard of. Besides all that there were shelves of old-fashioned food wafers. And all of the food was still edible. The labels testified that it had been preserved in ways that would make it last until an emergency made its use necessary. There had been no emergency since 1991, not the kind the Pasadena Chamber of Commerce had been thinking about.

In all there were five big rooms, each filled with food and assorted drink, including two still-functioning wells. Lembeck laughed as he made glancing inventories of the storehouse. He knew exactly what he would do now. That religious android had been right. When you had a purpose life was okay.

Lembeck took a look around the main room and then ran up the ramp corridor to the outer door.

He slammed the door shut and ran back inside.

He started to eat.

9

Muscadine

Feeling the tiny screws scattered underfoot in the dark hotel room, he stopped and said, "That nitwit. He's unscrewed one of his hands again and run off to send it to some damn nitwit girl."

Norm Gilroy flicked on the lights. The room was empty and he caught up the phone. While he was waiting for the desk, he knelt, holding the phone with his tilted head. He poked the rug, found a contact lens he'd lost over the week-end, and then located Muscadine's hand screws. Gilroy frowned and squinted at the things, dropped them in his pajama pocket. "Looks like his left hand this time. So he can still sign autographs."

"St. Thomas Hotel," said the night desk man.

Gilroy got his public relations voice back working. "Norm Gilroy. Have you seen Mr. Muscadine recently?" He must have left his chair and slipped out while Gilroy was taking his shower.

"Mr. Gilroy, Mr. Muscadine sped off in a taxi some ten or fifteen minutes ago."

"Uh, did you notice if he had his left hand stuck down in his coat pocket?"

"As a matter of fact, Mr. Gilroy, Mr. Muscadine didn't seem to have a left hand. He stopped at the desk to ask me where he could post a package at this hour."

"What did you tell him?"

"I suggested a mailbox," said the night man. "Has Mr. Muscadine's hand been injured due to some lack of thoughtfulness on the part of the hotel?"

"No," said Gilroy. "There's a rather tragic story behind it all, and I'm sure Mr. Muscadine would prefer that it remain a secret." Gilroy was on top of it now, handling it. He'd been in public relations a decade, with Muscadine nearly six years. "Thank you." He hung up.

That nitwit has gone out to mail his hand to that girl pacifist who plays the electrified sitar. As he plucked off his pajamas, Gilroy said, "You don't expect to run into an electric sitar-playing girl pacifist at an autographing session at The Emporium."

They were out of spares, too. Muscadine had sent one last week, air express, to that girl who placed third in the Miss Wyoming competition. That made six, seven, of the things. Dacoit & Sons was still conservative in many ways, a publishing house still headquartered in Boston. They wouldn't like all these hands cluttering up the mails. Gilroy hadn't told them yet. He was going to find out a few things in the Bay Area and then cope with Dacoit & Sons.

Gilroy pressed his round face where he thought his sinuses were, took a deep breath, buttoned his black spruce suit and went down to the lobby.

The pharmacist in the all-night drugstore just off the entrance hailed him. "Mr. Gilroy, I got it."

Muscadine's hand? "What?"

The druggist was small, gray toned with sprayed blond hair. "The cure for your case of San Francisco throat."

"Did you see Muscadine go by here?"

"Fifteen minutes back. In a cab heading up toward Nob Hill. He didn't seem to have any left hand. Is he sick?"

"It's just overwork."

"Sure, a best seller a year, I can imagine. Tell him I really loved the gondola stuff in *Consider This Small Dust!* a lot. I usually don't go for flagellation, but this was beautifully wrought." He lifted a small electric motor up onto his glass counter. "This is for your throat."

"How?"

"I devised it myself. Built from a paint sprayer I got at an unclaimed sale, combined with an insect squirter. You spray your throat with it three times a day."

"It's my nose now anyway," said Gilroy, backing.

"Sure, you've picked up San Francisco nose. It's a side effect from San Francisco throat. People come out here from New York, particularly people who live around East 65th and the East 70's, they always seem to get San Francisco throat, followed by San Francisco nose."

"I have to go find Muscadine," said Gilroy. But he returned to the counter. "You know, I do have an apartment on East 71st in New York."

"You didn't have to tell me, with your symptoms."

A foggy rain was hitting Union Square. Gilroy gave the St. Thomas doorman five dollars. "You know where Muscadine went?"

"He didn't give the cab driver a certain address," said the lumpy-uniformed man. His lower lip bulged under his chewing teeth. "Frankly, he spoke not too kindly to me, making remarks about how my uniform coat isn't the same color as my uniform pants. Which is only because I have the pants dry-cleaned Mondays. Of course, I read Muscadine's *Hence Vain Deluding Joys!* in the paperback. Being able to read between the lines, I'm not surprised to see that Muscadine drinks a lot."

"No, it's only that he gets a little touchy when he's been under pressure."

"Selling a million books a year wouldn't pressure me." The doorman narrowed one eye. "I think he may have headed for some all-night, after-hours place. Because he mentioned wanting to revel till dawn."

"Thanks." Gilroy bounced down into the taxi that had hissed up on the wet night street. "Some after hours clubs?" he said to the driver.

"Lots of people like Freddie's Jiveareeni Village," said the driver.

"That's kind of a dated name."

"They draw the more conservative, nostalgic crowd."

"We can start there," said Gilroy. He massaged his nose, watching the rain fall heavier.

At sunrise Gilroy was climbing up through a tangle of manzanita and rose bushes. He was across the Bay in Berkeley, high up in the hills. Dacoit & Sons had warned him to stay from Dr. Pragnell on all trips to the West Coast. But he hadn't located Muscadine in a long night of tracking. There was another autographing at Paul Elder's bookstore at noon and a talk-show interview at the dinner hour. Gilroy was hoping Leonard Pragnell could give him some kind of lead.

The Pragnell cottage didn't seem tall enough. It was roofed with shaggy shingles, encrusted with flowering vines. Gilroy knocked with the brass lion head.

The door whirred, buzzed and swung open inward.

"Your house is sinking into the ground, you know," said Gilroy while stepping into the hallway. Wicker chairs, about a dozen, were piled up against the left wall, with a fat calico cat slumped on the pinnacle.

"Has there been some fatality?" asked Dr. Pragnell's voice.

"Where's your speaker now? Used to be in the hat rack, under the eagle."

"Come on into the library. What's the tragedy?"

"He's missing. Can you suggest a way of finding him?" The library door whirred open. "He's not here? Quest for the father, return to the birthplace."

"Flapdoodle," said Dr. Pragnell. He was a Lincoln-shaped man, hunched in a wicker armchair.

The room was waist high in piles. Magazines, newspapers, paperbacks, phonograph records, overcoats, dress shirts and a miscellany. "I won't exactly report this visit to Dacoit & Sons," said Gilroy. "I have dropped them, as jovially as possible, a few hints about Muscadine's worsening state. Have you heard?"

Dr. Pragnell rotated his wide shoulders. "Muscadine's a sensitive machine, Norm. Much more complex than your television set, say, and think how many times some little thing goes wrong with that."

"Never. It's my Mercedes that's always on the fritz." He sat on a solid pile of *National Geographics*. "Muscadine has mailed his left hand off to a girl pacifist down at Big Sur."

His cheeks hollowing, the doctor said, "You have to build them a certain way, Norm. All his quirky sensitivity is linked with his creativity. You touch the public heart on the scale Muscadine does, and you have to have a few quirks. That's where the big boys, your IBMs and your Rands, that's where they went flooey. They refused to program in the quirks. As a result I am the only person so far to have built a functional, android-human shape robot who can write best-selling novels."

"Oh, so? We think now Little, Brown's got one, maybe two."

Pragnell tensed. "They can't. Perhaps by 1978, five years from now, maybe."

"Little, Brown, we hear, has got one intense girl novelist android and one faggot short-story writer," said Gilroy. "And you know that old lady British detective novelist who won the Edgar from the Mystery Writers of America last year? She died two years ago, and Simon & Schuster didn't tell anybody. They just replaced her with an android."

"I assure you it's only I who has broken through. Now, what's troubling you?"

"This Bay Area always makes Muscadine edgy, being near you, I think. It's much worse this trip. All over the country besides, things have been happening."

"Such as?"

"In Detroit he took to consuming forty cups of coffee a day, wandering around in the skid row and living on patent medicine. Then he tried to join the Merchant Marine, march in a protest against the war in Formosa and sign on as a fry cook. He almost married an automobile heiress, then threw her out of the second floor window of a motel in Hamtramck." Gilroy rubbed his nose. "I quieted that all down. In Chicago he'd go out only after dark, ordered the hotel suite lined with cork, had an affair with an actress nineteen years old, sat in on drums with the Muddy Waters band, got into a fist fight with a *Sun-Times* reporter, tried to run for assemblyman in Cicero and had himself photographed with his arm around the capo mafioso."

"Yes, all built into him," explained the doctor. "At times he'll think himself middle-aged and waning, others that he's an incurable drunkard. All done with microelectronics."

The calico cat strode in, yowled, and jumped onto Gilroy's back. Gilroy said, "Down in Los Angeles he snuck into Tijuana and fought two bulls under the name of Papa Muscadine. He rented a Cessna and flew the top lady gossip columnist in LA up to Vegas. Threw her out of the second floor window of a Del E. Webb development. I persuaded her not to sue, but we're dead as far as planting any more items in her column goes. In San Diego he challenged the Ku Klux Klan wizard to a fist fight, threw his hat in the ring as Conservative Party candidate for governor, tried to sign up a crew to trek with him on a lion-hunting safari to Africa, went on a three-day vodka and ginger beer binge, sent a telegram proposing marriage to the seventeen-year-old daughter of a former Senate majority leader and got himself nearly arrested in a paternity argument with a strip-teaser from Balboa who does her act dressed as Columbia, the Gem of the Ocean."

"All normal," said Dr. Pragnell. "When I built all those bits of creative talent and bestseller instinct into Muscadine, I also fed in all the wild, impulsive traits of the great men of letters, past and present."

"He's much worse now," said Gilroy. "The earlier nonsense, I manipulated into good publicity." He reached up behind his head and stroked the cat. "He's accelerating, on a collision course with himself. He keeps dismantling parts and shipping them to girls he gets interested in. What's more unsettling, Muscadine's talking more and more about how he's betraying his talent. About ending the mockery in suicide."

"I would think," said Pragnell, "that the success of his recent books, *Fair Daffodils, We Weep!* and *Our Bugles Sang Truce!*, would lift him out of the slough."

"The last two books were nothing much," said Gilroy. "I thought Jocelyn from Dacoit & Sons was sending you royalty statements. *Bugles* hardly did 100,000 copies. Not one book club deal or movie offer, and the TV series we were talking never jelled. Muscadine's sliding down."

"He can't, he's a machine. He'll go on forever."

"No author lasts forever," said Gilroy. "Muscadine keeps telling me all the great writers go to pieces at forty, and he's got the idea that's his age. He sings in an Irish brogue at times, says he'll be taken off by the Lady of the Lake, a victim of a weak chest."

"You don't sound so good yourself."

"It's that fog in SF. How about Muscadine and where he might be?"

"I imagine he'll be back at the hotel by the time you get back to San Francisco," said Pragnell. "There's a homing device built into him. Before you end your stay here, bring Muscadine over, and I'll perhaps tinker a little."

"You know," said Gilroy, "if he keeps dismantling himself somebody's going to tumble he's an android. The Authors' League won't be happy."

"Muscadine is the first wave of the sea of the future."

"In ten years maybe. Right now the bad press could ruin Dacoit & Sons."

"I'll make a few simple adjustments on him, Norm. Don't worry."

"I'll need a new left hand for him."

Reaching back to a shelf, Pragnell got a paper sack and tossed it. "A pair in there and extra screws."

Gilroy detached the calico cat and left. He sneezed all the way downhill.

The blues singer, heavy and with dark glasses, was sitting on his bed. The luggage rack held a slim, rangy blonde girl of about twenty. On the floor, his hand behind his tight-curled dark head, was Muscadine.

Gilroy said, closing the hotel room door quietly, "Is that a blues singer on my bed?"

"One of these mornings," sang the Negro with his steel-stringed guitar, "that black chariot is going to come for me. Uh huh."

"That's," said Muscadine, "none other than Blind Sunflower Slim himself, it is."

Gilroy scowled down at him. "Oh, hell, where's your right eye?"

"Buried with the dead past," said Muscadine, sitting up.

The blonde girl said, "He lost it at the Neither/Nor Club out on Divisadero Street. I'm Jean Pinajian from the San Francisco *Post-Enquirer*, and I was out there with a date and recognized Mr. Muscadine, who was sitting in on electrified harmonica, and asked for an exclusive interview."

"I saw a whole tray full of glass eyes when I picked up my new contacts," said Gilroy. "It'll be okay. Miss Pinajian, we'll be happy to let you have an exclusive interview tomorrow first thing. Right now, I think Mr. Muscadine should rest." Actually the android never had to rest. He was supposed to sit quietly in a chair while Gilroy slept, but lately he wouldn't always.

The girl nodded. "He's so tortured. Slim, let's go."

The blues singer left the bed, opened the door for the girl reporter and they both left.

Gilroy reached into the paper sack he'd brought. "I got you a new hand. Don't go sending it away to some peace protester."

"Peace," said Muscadine. He grabbed the new hand and absently screwed it to his wrist. "I'll know it soon. The river of forgetfulness flows out to sea and at last weary Lethe comes home to roost."

"Will you promise to stay here while I run down and buy you an eye?"

Muscadine rumpled his curly hair with his newly installed hand. "Washed up, Norman. The old greatness is gone, even the near greatness. Once I hoped I'd be allowed to express what I feel it is my mission to say and not be forced to repeat what the poor mindless mob wants to be told. I was happy as a boy in Wales or Baltimore, wherever it was. When I had that bicycle and helped with the harvest and had to shoot my horse when he fell into the canyon and walked the October street smelling the old year die and sat on the street car that ran by the Mississippi. Gone, tossed by the wind, the past. Dead, as soon I'll be."

"Calm down," said Gilroy. "Sit yourself on one of the beds. We'll put fresh clothes on you and get over to the book store."

"I got a feeling this morning that black chariot is coming for me," sang Muscadine.

Gilroy could hear it out waiting for the elevator.

The Topless Tower was on the eighth floor of a building in North Beach. There were seven people dining in the big dining room, five naked waitresses. A thin, ragged man named Cullen Frimmer did his nightly talk-and-phone show from a back booth.

Gilroy and Muscadine were with Frimmer, waiting. The headache commercial ended and Frimmer said into his mike, "We were chatting, before that intrusion, with Neil Muscadine, author of *Consider This Small Dust!* and other such crap. I was telling Mr. Muscadine I find his work godawful. We're taking calls now from any of you who want to speak to Muscadine."

Muscadine was drinking boilermakers. Dr. Pragnell had constructed him so that he could appear to eat and drink and show the effects.

The manager of the Tower, a round man in a tuxedo, rushed up and slid Gilroy a note. The note said, "Tell him in his ear don't say crap. Remember the FCC."

Muscadine read the note while Gilroy did, and said, "Remember the FCC."

Frimmer was drinking sweet vermouth. "Crap to the FCC."

The phone at his left buzzed and he picked it up. "This is the lonely old lady of Presidio Heights."

"Now what?"

"That Muscadine. God bless him, I know that voice. Ask him was he ever abandoned on the steps of a church in Youngstown, Ohio, many years ago."

"What kind of crap is this?" asked Frimmer.

The Tower manager grabbed at Frimmer. "I told you don't say crap on the radio anymore from my Candlelight and Wine Room, you foulmouth bastard."

Muscadine got the phone. "I was indeed that waif, ma'am. I am your own beloved son, mother."

"Skippy," said the woman. "After four decades."

Frimmer tipped the table candle and tried to ignite the

manager's tuxedo. The manager hit him in the ear. "I'm sorry to involve Mr. Muscadine in this," he asided to Gilroy.

"I'm sending you something, mother," Muscadine said into the phone. He spun off his left hand, using his steak knife on the tiny screws. "And something else."

Gilroy was blocked by the table from stopping Muscadine. "Easy," he said. "Talk about the book."

Muscadine took off his right foot and set it on the table. "Where are you now, mother?"

"Out on Clay Street, near the kiddie playground. Will you be coming home to me, Skippy?"

"No, I'm going to a better home than this world dreams of. The world is too much with me, what with one thing and another." Muscadine jumped up. "I'm going down slow, goodbye, goodbye." He ran in a rickety lopsided way out of the room.

Gilroy hung up the phone and chased him.

Down in the street the chase involved cabs, foggy hills, the Golden Gate Bridge. Muscadine finally stopped beyond the town of Sausalito, near an unsettled stretch of wooded countryside that hung over the dark Bay. He left the cab and went running through the trees.

Gilroy paid his cab and sent it away. No use having any more witnesses to Muscadine's displays. The other cab headed back for the city, and Gilroy began working down-hill through the sharp trees.

Muscadine was strewn all along the beach. Arms, the other foot, legs, a tangle of miniaturized parts. All scattered over the grey damp sand.

Muscadine's curly head was at the water's edge. "The shore of oblivion," he said.

"You nitwit. How'd you get yourself dismantled so damn fast?"

"My powers have failed, I'm a disappointment to my mother, the little lady of Presidio Heights. It is finished." The head hopped into the dark water.

When Gilroy reached it the head was sinking, giving off sparks and frizzling sounds.

Gilroy put the two cardboard boxes he'd found behind a Sausalito supermarket down next to Dr. Pragnell's cat. "I didn't bother to go back to the radio show for the other hand and foot."

The doctor said, "I tuned in on the interview. Perhaps I overprogrammed Muscadine. When we put him together again I'll fiddle some, hold back."

Gilroy sat again on the *Geographics*. "You're a medical doctor, too, aren't you?"

"Surely."

"You can sign a death certificate."

"On whom?"

Gilroy pointed a foot at the two cartons. One had Gallo Wine printed on its sides in red. "He's used up most of his best stuff in the six bestsellers we had." Gilroy coughed. "His popularity's been dropping badly the past year. One of the reasons for such an intensive tour, this book."

"Simply kinks which can be fixed."

"You get only five percent of the Muscadine earnings," said Gilroy. "Could you build a machine, not an android, just one that sits there and writes what we want? One to do us a few books we can split fifty-fifty on. Dacoit & Sons will be mad, but they can't do anything without admitting Muscadine was a robot. After this, you can always build a new android."

"What do you want the writing machine for, Norm?"

"I'm associated with Muscadine in the minds of a lot of people, especially reviewers and critics," said Gilroy. "First you sign a death certificate on him. Announce he passed on suddenly, hinting at acute alcoholism with complications."

"Then?"

"Then we write *My Years with Muscadine*," said Gilroy.

"Followed by *The Day Muscadine Died* and *The Picture Life of Muscadine*."

Dr. Pragnell picked up his cat and patted it. "It could be done."

Gilroy nodded at the boxes, tilted back. "If I stay in California for a while, somebody's going to have to come up with a cure for my respiratory problems."

"It could be done," Dr. Pragnell told him.

10

Disposal

He couldn't eat any more of the haddock schnitzel. Lon
Snowden nudged the sample container over to the left side
of the dining area table and reached into his briefcase. The
next sample to be tested was labeled cod jubilee in the
chief's lopsided printing. Lon didn't like to bring food home
from the office but the preliminary response figures on
eleven new—he glanced at his watch: nearly midnight—Seawise Processed Seafoods was due tomorrow before coffee
break 1.

Fog was resting heavy against the shuttered window of
the dining area. Victorian Village was thick with fog
tonight, most nights. Lon pried open the cod container,
made a note with a grease pencil on a blue response punchcard. He was thirty-four—he glanced at his watch: five past
midnight—and already he was but two moves away from
being a Senior Food Tester for Seawise. As Ryan Kubert,

the only guy at Seawise he almost trusted, had said at lunch several times, being a Senior Food Tester was a good thing. Ryan was four moves from it.

When Lon was rushed, as tonight, he never bothered to heat the foods he was responding to. That didn't seem to affect his judgment. Rolling another bite of cod around in his mouth, he blacked in the square next to the Terrible response. He shoved the rest of the sample over with the nine he'd run through since Maya had gone into the sleeping area. Before he tried the eel brittle he'd stand up—he glanced at his watch: quarter after twelve—and stretch.

Terry, their younger boy, was watching him from the entrance to the children's sleep section. "What's the matter?" Lon mouthed.

"Some day," said Terry, "I'll be boss around here. You'll be among the first to get it. Quick, like that."

Terry was four. The death threat business was something he was going through. "Back to bed," Lon told him softly. The office psychiatrist said feeling hostile toward the father figure was okay.

"First pull your fingers off, one by one," said the little boy. "Then the toes. Lastly, the nose."

"Get the hell into bed or I'll break your damn arm." Lon glanced at his watch: twenty-one past twelve.

Terry obeyed.

Lon found his stomach mint capsules in his briefcase, quickly swallowed two. Then he got back to the eel brittle. It was Bland and Delicious, he decided.

By one he had everything tested. Somehow fog had seeped into the dining area and was hanging low to the rug. As Lon walked into the kitchen with all the scraps of seafood the mist tattered. He got the light control with his elbow, sidestepped to the porthole of the disposal unit. "Grind away," he said and both-handed all the containers and fish scraps into the hole.

A new and not appropriate sound came out of the wall

disposal. The unit made a sound like packages of metal washers dropping off the back of a truck, then a grating cat wail. Twenty-nine seconds of silence and then all the garbage was thrown back out of the hole.

Lon gathered it up in a lemon yellow refuse pan and shot it back through the porthole.

The disposal made the same new sounds, and an out-of-tune guitar twang, and threw the garbage out again. The leftovers from Lon's testing plus the leavings from dinner.

"It's on the fritz," he said.

Finally he found an empty container big enough to hold all the rejected garbage. He didn't know what to do with it. He left it in the kitchen and went to bed. In the morning Maya would know.

Maya, with a metronome motion of her hand, put eggshells into a blue plyfilm bag. "We can store it in the utility closet until the disposal's fixed."

Lon flathanded the legs of the turned-off cleaning android aside and wedged the box of last night's garbage into the narrow utility compartment. "I guess."

The Victorian Village school cruiser chimed outside and Pete, the six-year-old, ran from the kitchen.

Terry got up from the breakfast nook with his half-finished bowl of protein mash and said, "I want to put my garbage in the hole."

"Disposal's busted," said Lon. "You can't. Put it there by mommy."

"I want to put it in the hole."

"Well, you can't."

Terry frowned. "When I take over this place I won't forget all this. First we'll stretch you, then compress you. Crack, crack your bones will go. Snap, snap."

"Go to your room," said Lon.

"Not a room, it's an area," said Terry, going.

"A phase." Maya set the bag of breakfast garbage in the

closet. "Shall I call Mr. Goodwagon at the Victorian Village office?"

Lon checked the wall clock. Fourteen minutes before he he had to be at the San Francisco tube. "I'll do it." In the phone alcove he smoothed his pale hair, sat down, dialed Goodwagon.

"Well, aren't you the early riser," said the secretary android who appeared on the screen.

"Mr. Goodwagon, please."

"He's on the links."

"Oh. Well, look. Our disposal isn't working. Victorian Village's Maintenance Department is supposed to fix it, isn't it?"

"Of course. No one else is allowed to tamper with VV equipment. Read your lease."

"Okay. When exactly could you have somebody over to fix the thing?"

The android said, "September 14 at 2:30."

Lon looked at his wristwatch. "Yes, but this is Ausust 26, 8:14."

"8:16," corrected the android. "Otherwise you're right."

"What do we do with our garbage until September?"

"Don't throw it in the street," said the android. "That's against state, federal and Victorian Village law. Don't bury it. That's illegal, too."

"What would you suggest?"

"I'll switch you to Dr. Wigransky, our staff trouble shooter."

Dr. Wigransky, when he came on the screen, was naked. "Yes?"

"We have," said Lon, looking away, "this problem about our garbage."

"You can't seem to look me in the eye."

"Your eye maybe. It's the rest of you."

"You call so early you can't expect formal attire. Lots of business stress?"

"Sure, but the problem is we have this disposal that won't work and they can't come and fix it till the middle of next month and I was wondering what we were supposed to do."

"How old are you?"

"Thirty-four. Why?"

"Thirty-four years old and native born from the way you talk and you don't know what to do with a little garbage."

"It's not a little. By next month it'll be a lot. I'm a food tester, I bring a great deal of food home to work on."

"That's an interesting field," said Dr. Wigransky, who had slipped on a polo shirt while Lon hadn't been watching him. "I have a brother who's a wastrel. Maybe you could get him into food testing."

"I don't have much influence," Lon told him. "What about our garbage?"

"Call Sayffertitz."

"Sayffertitz?"

"The last of the scavengers." Dr. Wigransky blacked off.

The vintage dump truck drove up onto their small lawn at a little after nine that evening. From the realeather driver's seat leaped a tanned man in a tweed jumpsuit. He had a moustache, shoulder-length black hair and a malacca stick. He hit the chime buzzer with a gloved thumb.

"Sayffertitz," he told Maya when she opened the door.

"Oh, yes. We understand you still pick up garbage."

Sayffertitz handed her his cane, eased off his gloves. "I am the only remaining scavenger in the San Francisco Bay Area. People depend on disposal units now. However, as you've just learned, disposals do break down. Then you have to come to Sayffertitz."

Lon had been sitting in the living area, sampling. He stood now as Maya led Sayffertitz in. "When will you pick up the garbage?"

Sayffertitz sat down on a plystool. "You people amuse me. I haven't agreed to haul your garbage yet. Tell me about it and I'll see if I can take on your account. Do you have any brandy?"

"Maya, get Mr. Sayffertitz a brandy."

Sayffertitz' left eye was not quite the same shade of green as his right. He fixed it on Lon, tossed his hair once. "Just what sort of garbage is it you'd like me to consider?"

"Garbage," said Lon. "Household stuff."

The scavenger stroked one tweedy knee. "What's that in front of you there?"

"My work. I'm a food tester."

"But what is it specifically?"

"Well," said Lon, pointing in turn, "terrapin flambé, shrimp jellyroll, chicken fried halibut and anchovy bisque."

"You intend to include that stuff in my garbage?" asked Sayffertitz. He dropped to the rug, approaching the coffee table on hands and knees. "Which is the halibut again?"

"The orange stuff. It's artificially colored."

Sayffertitz sniffed. "I don't know. You people. Boy, you want me to toss that kind of thing into my truck. That's an awfully persistent odor."

"Seafood. It does have a sort of oceany smell."

"You're used to it. Numbed by your job."

"What days do you pick up? Is there a regular schedule or what?"

Sayffertitz rubbed his lighter eye. "You people." He stretched up, scratched his stomach. "I service my clients in this area on Tuesday mornings at the moment."

"Next week then?"

"Next week. Tuesday morning at 7 a.m." He bent to sniff the halibut again. "I don't know if I can accept you people or not."

"We'll pay well," said Maya, offering him a brandy on a bronzed tray.

"My fee is ten dollars per pickup. In advance."

"Ten dollars?" asked Lon.

"In advance. If I accept the account." He touched the tip

of his nose with the brandy glass rim. "Do you have a scale?"

"In the bathroom."

"Remember this then. No more than five pounds of garbage per Tuesday."

"Then you accept us?" said Maya.

"This brandy is not too bad." He drank it down. "Tuesday, seven promptly. No more than five pounds. In boxes. On the left side of the lawn facing the street." He took the money Lon held out, bowed slightly. He went to the door and let himself out into the fog.

Lon picked up the container of halibut and inhaled.

Sayffertitz didn't show up on the following Tuesday. Nor Wednesday. Thursday at 8:17, with nine cartons of garbage stacked in the corner of the cruiser port, Lon called the scavenger. That morning Sayffertitz didn't answer. On Friday he did but he was unhappy that Lon was waking him at 8:14 on his day off. Lon apologized.

Sayffertitz said, "You people and your fish. I refuse to accept any further garbage from you."

"What do you mean any further? I gave you ten bucks and you . . ."

The scavenger went to black.

Using fog as a cover Lon was able, that night, to toss one carton of garbage into a public disposal at the nearest cul-de-sac. The unit was labeled: For leaves and fallen greenery only. Friday it worked but Saturday the mist was thinner and a mounted android policer, who had been watching from a shadowy gazebo, caught Lon and fined him twenty-two dollars.

Maya found she could flush eggshells and coffee grounds down the toilet. The bowl balked at anything else. Lon dumped four cartons the next Monday night at the beach some eighteen miles from their home. The litter patrol caught him on the third trip and that resulted in a seventy-three-dollar fine and the revoking of his sunbathing privileges for a ninety-day period. He was able, by pretending to be strewing the ashes of a loved one, to get rid of three cartons flying low over the Pacific Ocean in his cruiser at sundown. You couldn't do that more than once a month, though.

By the end of August they had twenty-one cartons of garbage in their gingerbread house. When no more would fit in the small cruiser port Maya started putting refuse in the recreation area cupboards. The house now had a quiet soursweet odor most of the time and Terry threatened to have his father pulled asunder by draft horses if the smell didn't stop. Lon called the Bay Area Health Authority but they said they couldn't help him until he had either maggots or plague-carrying rats in his garbage.

He discovered he could get rid of about a half a pound a day by carrying it to work in his briefcase and tossing it in the office disposal when the machine was not being watched. Maya had meanwhile been taking a carton a day over to Carole and Robert, their friends two blocks away. Carole and Robert couldn't dispose of more because the first time Maya had tried to get rid of several cartons at once and the Victorian Village authorities had warned Carole against overloading her appliances again. They knew three other couples in the development and gradually, by using all of their friends' disposal units and with Lon sneaking the more unobtrusive garbage into the office, they got down to only ten cartons stored in the cruiser area.

On the first Tuesday in September, Terry decided to drop his left shoe in their disposal hole. The unit roared and thrashed for three and a quarter minutes and then started kicking back. Out came eggshells, orange peels, coconut shreds, soft drink bulbs, teabags, hambones, fishtails, kleenex, back issue magazines, green marbles, cabbage, bandaids, protein loaf, plyogloves, rose petals, tuna fish, melon rinds, a dead canary and Terry's shredded shoe. The kitchen area was a foot awash with old garbage before the machine stopped rejecting.

"Okay," said Lon when it sputtered and stopped. "That's it. I'm going to bury the stuff." He strode into the cruiser area and grabbed up the power shovel.

It was dark and misty. He turned on the lawn spotlights and began to dig. He had a pit about seven inches deep and three feet wide dug when the live Victorian Village cop cruised down with his android assistant.

"What are you up to, Mr. Snowden?" asked the cop.

"Burying garbage."

"No, now," said the VV cop. "That's an infraction."

"The whole house is possessed by the stuff," Lon told him. "Besides which I'm starting to feel an enormous guilt over this."

"But you people shouldn't dig up your lawn."

Lon threw the shovel at him.

Victorian Village didn't have its own jail completed yet so Lon was put in the city jail in nearby Sunnyvale. The judge let him off with a $500 fine and twelve days in jail. Maya told him, on his third day in the cell, that since he'd assaulted a Victorian Village staff member the tract people were considering evicting them and had, in the meantime, put their name at the end of the waiting list for repairs. That meant no disposal repairs would be made until October 2nd.

In jail Lon dreamt a great deal about garbage. And he got to know a man in the next cell named Blind John Dove. Blind John said he was one of the few blind private investigators in the San Francisco Bay Area and he solved his cases with his sense of smell.

Lon explained his garbage problem and Blind John, a fat freckled man with a strip of green plyoglass across his upper face, said, "I know what you can do."

"What?"

"Playland. Near Playland over in Frisco there's an old bath house that's closed up. By the ocean. From the street level it's three floors down inside. All gutted out. Lots of people with garbage problems throw things there. No guards at night. That part of the city's hardly frequented any more. Load your cruiser. Fly."

After his release Lon went back to Seawise and found he no longer had his job. That same evening he and Maya, with the house still cluttered with nineteen cartons of garbage Maya hadn't been able to get rid of yet with the neighbors, had a quarrel. Maya took Terry and Pete and walked over to Carole and Robert's to spend the night.

Lon sat in the kitchen area for a while. He was hungry but if he ate it would only mean more garbage. At 10:16 he started loading boxes of garbage into the cruiser. It was a chill, foggy night and he put on a realfleece jacket. He got all the garbage, except for a handful of burnt marshmallows that fell and eluded him in a corner, stowed in the ship.

He took off for the city. By eleven he was parked uphill from the long deserted public bath house. He quietly carried an armload of garbage up to the marble steps, climbed down and pushed the doors open. They skittered back and he was looking down on a cool hollow. There was a sweet sour musty damp smell here. Lon heaved the first batch of cartons. Heard them hit seconds later and bounce on some kind of loose metal.

A wind was rising out across the ocean and it blew the lid off one of the cartons on the next load. In twenty-two minutes he was at the pit edge with the last three boxes. He threw them, listened as they hit, bounced, settled.

A truck cut off behind him in the street, leaping feet hit the misted pavement. "You people," said a voice. "Encroaching on one of my private dump spots. It's difficult enough to survive in our society without people like you."

Lon turned and watched Sayffertitz approach.

"The fish man," grinned the scavenger. "Well, climb

down there and retrieve whatever it is you've thrown. You
poacher." He pointed at the pit with his malacca cane.

Lon bobbed, caught the stick away from him. He hit him
several times over the skull with it. Sayffertitz slumped.
Lon flung the stick into the pit. He stooped and grabbed
two holds on the tweed jumpsuit. He braced himself and
pitched Sayffertitz into the dark hollow.

He didn't stay to hear him land.

11

To the Rescue

The opcruiser rocked down gently onto the sand and then skittered into a protecting scatter of brush. The controller's chair tilted Bill Herriman ahead so that the view tube that was lowering from the ceiling would just meet his eyes.

"Which cottage?" Bill asked the cruiser. Across the small calm bay was the town of Artesian, one of the several similar beach towns on the planet Tarragon.

"The blue one with red shingles," said the cruiser. "That was in Report 540–46, you know."

"I forgot," said Bill, studying the house where the client's daughter was supposed to be staying.

The cruiser flicked on one of the canned pep talks. "Mult/Op is the largest private investigating service in any known universe," said the speaker grid under Bill's chair, "because it employs the best equipment and the best men." A Mult/Op march was played.

"Down on the volume," said Bill. Mult/Op's Mechanical Wing had tracked Maxwell Outbanner's runaway daughter to this town on Tarragon. It was Bill's job, aided by his opcruiser, to keep an eye on the synthetics heiress and to subtly extricate her from whatever situation she was in and get her back to her home planet of Barnum.

"Have a drink," said the cruiser.

The bottom drawer of Bill's realwood desk slid out and a fifth of bourbon stood up.

"Not at eleven in the morning."

The cruiser poured him a shot in a tumbler. "Have a drink."

Bill let the bourbon sit on the file cabinet next to him. A rangy blonde had come out on the sun area of the watched cottage. She had long tan legs and was wearing a yellow shift. "That's Marj Outbanner, huh?"

"Have a drink," said the cruiser. It poured another.

"Come on," said Bill. "Don't go on the fritz again."

A brown wide man with considerable body hair had joined the runaway heiress on the sundeck.

"He's pretty tough looking for a ceramicist," said Bill.

"Have a drink," said the cruiser.

Four shots of bourbon were lined up on the cabinet.

"Damn it," said Bill. He stood up and went to the file cabinet which held the opcruiser repair manual. The damn cruiser had broken down once already since he'd arrived on Tarragon. That was why he'd been a day late getting here to watch Marj Outbanner.

"Here's looking at you," said the cruiser, pouring bourbon into the view tube.

"Stop it," said Bill. The drawer with the manual in it was stuck shut. Bill kicked the cabinet.

"Oof," said the cruiser.

The bottle fell into the dictadesk and all the lights in the cabin went out.

"May day," said the cruiser in a gay falsetto.

The emergency exit popped open and smoke began to come out of the R&I machine.

"Hellsfire," said Bill. He dived out onto the yellow beach. While he stood looking at the smoking cruiser a motorboat jumped out of the water and shot across the sand. It slammed into the cruiser's rear end, scattering silver paint flakes and taillight shards.

"Darn," said the boatman, a curly blond man. "Boat went out of control. My fault. I'll get you a repair man on my com. My fault."

"Have a drink," said the cruiser.

The cruiser repair shop was in the town of Artesian, about five blocks from the ceramacist's cottage where Marj Outbanner was going astray.

"This is a real honor," said Ernest Piute, the head mechanic. He was small and round, dotted with blue-grey grease spots.

"I was hoping you'd fix it right on the beach there," Bill said.

Piute shook his head. "Have to tow these exceptional ones in," he said. "I don't dare tamper with a machine of the caliber of a Mult/Op cruiser right out on a dirty beach."

The cruiser sat on a rack in the middle of the cool shadowy repair shop. Next to it a man with mismatched socks was lying under an ice cream cruiser.

"What do you think's wrong?" Bill asked Piute.

"Can't tell yet," said the mechanic. "But I'd guess it was your Central Diagramming Center."

"Can you fix it?"

"Sure," nodded Piute. "But these opcruisers use an eccentric CD Center and I'd have to get a new one teleported from Barnum."

"How long?"

"I know you're probably in the midst of a caper," said Piute. "Tomorrow morning?"

Bill grunted. "Not sooner?"

"I have to relocate your whole Control Housing, not to mention taking up the rug and moving floor lamps. And the rear fender has to be replaced. You don't want to go around looking crumpled."

"I hide a lot," said Bill. "It really doesn't matter."

Piute smiled. "Don't worry. I'll mend that while we're waiting for the CD Center to get here. I'll put your job on top priority, stick two crack men on it. Eric and Manfred. That's Manfred under the ice cream wagon."

"Can I get some gear out of the storage compartment?" Bill's portable listening equipment was in there.

"Nope. That storage door froze when the motor boat hit you."

"Well, okay. I'll check with you this afternoon."

"I'll have you mobile again by tomorrow early," Piute called as Bill hurried away on foot.

The palm tree next to the cottage barely concealed Bill. He hunched himself small and strained his ears to hear.

"Let's," said Marj Outbanner from the sundeck.

The burly ceramicist chuckled. "Let's at once, Marj."

"We won't have to pack much. It'll be a quick honeymoon."

Bill groaned internally.

"Right," said the ceramicist. "Really little more than a weekend at Calamari and then back here."

"Wonderful."

"Overwhelming."

"Love."

"Darling."

"Oh, boy," thought Bill. They were eloping to Calamari, the big gambling and marrying resort town five hundred miles across the desert.

"Get started packing," Marj said.

"You, too, sweet."

Bill knew their client would want this marriage stopped. He jumped up and vaulted the blue wall around the sun deck.

"Who are you?" asked the rangy blonde as he landed.

"Herriman of Mult/Op Detective Agency," Bill told her. "I suggest you reconsider, Miss Outbanner. Your father, who has hired us, would not approve of this rash move of yours." Actually the ceramicist didn't look like such a bad guy. However, in this job, which Bill had held for over two years, it was best to follow orders. Thinking didn't pay.

"Like hell," said Marj.

The big ceramicist picked up a ceramic owl and hit Bill over the head with it. "Here's for you, shamus."

When Bill awoke it was twilight and the cottage was long empty.

Back at the repair Ernest Piute announced, "It wasn't so bad as we thought. It's all fixed and ready to fly."

That meant the eloping Marj Outbanner would only have a two or three hour lead. He should be able to overtake them in the fast opcruiser. "Great," said Bill, heading for the cruiser.

"Wait," said Piute. "You've got to sign the credit forms."

Just at nightfall Bill took off and headed across the desert for Calamari.

The cruiser said, "Oh oh."

"What?" mumbled Bill. He'd been dozing in his swivel chair.

"Mechanical Scrutiny reports that a man named Norman L. Vision is tailing Marj Outbanner and Culligan, the ceramicist."

"Who's Vision?"

"It's in R&I."

"Save time and tell me."

"He's believed the head of a gang of kidnappers."

"That's just great," said Bill. "Where does Scrutiny make Marj and that Culligan?"

"Their rental cruiser is just arriving in Calamari."

"We're how far?"

"It's on the log."

"Tell me."

"One hundred miles. A half hour."

"Good," said Bill. He caught his elbows and closed his eyes.

"Flecker, Nathan, five foot three, asterisk shaped scar over left knee," said the cruiser, bouncing oddly. "Also known as Nathan Faith, Nat Flecker and Lightfoot Riley. Specializes in greenhouse robberies."

"What's all this?" asked Bill.

"Flennoy, Walter R., alias Little Wally, five foot eleven, color blind in the left eye. Oops." The cruiser turned a somersault and began gliding down toward the desert.

"Hey," said Bill, trying to untangle himself from the contents of his In box.

"Flerrings, Fleswinger, Flettsman, Flocker, Floodstein," said the cruiser. It became silent and then there was a great thumping sound.

"Blast," said Bill. They'd crashed on the dark desert. The repair manual was accessible this time and he began checking out the ship.

A rough half hour later someone knocked on his door.

Keeping his place, Bill went over and looked out.

"Are you in trouble?" It was a slender redhaired girl, and behind her a short square man.

"Who are you?" Bill asked through the door.

"I'm Priscilla Lincross, assistant to Dr. Ralph Deeping."

"Hi," said Dr. Deeping.

"We've been conducting a motivational research study in the village over there," explained Priscilla. "As we were returning to our cruiser we noticed your fallen craft. Are you in trouble?"

Bill got the door open. "I can't seem to get my cruiser functioning. Everything checks out. It won't work, though." He looked past the girl and said to Dr. Deeping. "Are you good with machines?"

"I'm the leading machine psychologist on Tarragon," said Deeping. "I'm an ace motivational research man, too, and not bad at analyzing people. You, for instance, seem anxiety ridden."

Bill told them about the case he was on, about Marj Outbanner's elopement with Culligan and about the possibility of a kidnap attempt by a man named Norman L. Vision.

"I'll check out your ship and see what's wrong," said the doctor.

Priscilla climbed in and Dr. Deeping followed.

"Would anybody like a drink?" asked the cruiser.

"Don't intrude," said Bill.

The compact Dr. Deeping prowled the cruiser, poking it and asking it questions. After fifteen minutes he said, "An interesting case, Mr. Herriman."

"Oh, so?"

"Do you have a pair of dice?"

"In the drawer with the bourbon."

Deeping fetched the dice, handed them to Bill, said, "Do you think you could control these?"

"No."

"Try for a seven."

Bill threw them on the desk top. "Seven," he said.

"Exactly," said Dr. Deeping.

Priscilla had put on a pair of large round-rimmed glasses. She cocked them slightly on her nose and said, "You're not really happy with the Mult/Op detective people, Bill."

"Sure, I am."

"He majored in psych in college," said the cruiser. "His uncle got him into Mult/Op."

"Shut up," said Bill. "I like detective work. It keeps me in the open, moving around, meeting people."

"Mr. Herriman," said Dr. Deeping, "ours has been a fortunate, though chance, meeting."

"He's diagnosed your problem," explained the redhead.

"Oh yeah? In fifteen minutes?"

"It's not difficult," said Deeping. "This ship of yours is the obvious victim of telekinetic reprisal."

"Meaning?"

"You have extrasensory abilities," Dr. Deeping said. "You basically resent your job and your cruiser. It is you, Mr. Herriman, who have been putting it on the blink. This is not the first failure of the ship, is it?"

"No, I've had trouble with it the past few months."

"Increasing trouble?"

"Well, yes. In fact, yesterday a motor boat came up out of the water and hit us."

"Exactly," said Deeping.

"I did that, too?"

"Of course."

Bill shook his head. "I don't believe it. Anyway, whatever caused the trouble? How can we fix it?"

"It's your Central Diagramming Center. You've bollixed it," said Deeping as he patted the cruiser wall. "Ship will have to be towed in."

"Hell! That Vision guy will kidnap Marj Outbanner before we catch up."

"We're," said Priscilla, "leaving for Calamari in a few minutes. You're welcome to a ride."

"Let me get my portable equipment so I can stay in contact with Mechanical Scrutiny."

Dr. Deeping stroked the cruiser wall.

Wiping grease from his face Dr. Deeping said, "It's not as bad as your cruiser."

Bill was standing next to the doctor's fallen black cruiser, not looking at Priscilla in the doorway. "You think I did this to your cruiser, too?"

"Beyond a doubt," said Deeping. "There's strong evidence of telekinetic energy expenditures."

"Can you fix it?"

"It'll take two hours but yes."

It was bright midmorning when the Deeping cruiser sailed across the outskirts of the vastly neon Calamari.

"Mechanical Scrutiny reports the Outbanner girl and Culligan have just entered a chapel in the tower of the Lucky Mojo Hotel on Sheridan Street," said Bill. "Can you drop me there?"

"Certainly," said Dr. Deeping.

"What about your kidnapper, Vision?" asked Priscilla.

"Actually," said Bill. "Actually, the scrutinizer that was watching him is sort of haywire and I'm not getting reports at the moment."

"You'll be careful?" said the redhaired girl.

Dr. Deeping dropped the cruiser down in front of the Lucky Mojo. "Priscilla works with me at my home. Visit us when you've wound up this assignment."

Bill ran from the cruiser and into the hotel. "Marriage chapel?" he asked an android bellhop.

"Elevators 22–26, sir. Floor 40."

"Thanks."

"Welcome to the Lucky Mojo Hotel," said his elevator.

"Floor 40," said Bill.

He and a bearded man with a plaid yarmulke were alone in the car.

The elevator closed and rose.

"I notice," said the bearded man, "grease spots on your tunic. Are you mechanically inclined?"

"No," replied Bill.

After a moment the elevator said, "Mojo. Mojo. Mojo." It stopped just after the number panel flashed 39.

"Damn," said Bill. "Let's ring the emergency bell."

"No need," said the bearded man. "We'll pry the roof off and climb the cable to 40."

"Yeah?"

"Here, give me a boost." With agile swiftness, though he dropped his yarmulke once, the bearded man got the roof slot open and himself and Bill out on top of the elevator.

"Now what?" asked Bill.

"Rudy, Sky?" called the man, cupping his hands. "Are you there?"

"Huh, chief?"

"I'm down here in the elevator shaft. Get those doors up there pried open."

"Okay, chief."

"Are you bound for the wedding?" asked the bearded man as they shinnied up the cable.

"I'm trying to stop the wedding and a possible kidnapping. I'm with Mult/Op," said Bill. "Are you here for the wedding?"

"No," said the man as he stepped through the sprung doors of the shaft. "I'm Norman L. Vision. I'm here for the kidnapping."

He helped Bill into the corridor and then knocked him unconscious with a sockful of coins.

The getaway cruiser had green tinted windows. When Bill awoke they were over the middle of downtown Calamari.

Sitting next to him on the broad rear seat was Marj Outbanner, bound and gagged. Next to her a trussed-up Culligan.

Norman L. Vision, beardless now, sat in a lounging chair with a stun rod on his lap. "My finest hour," he said to Bill. "An exceptional kidnapping, with a bonus hostage."

Bill wondered if Dr. Deeping was right about his ability to fritz machines. Now was a good time to try it. He gritted his teeth and closed his eyes.

The cruiser continued its flight.

Bill kept trying.

The cruiser's radio began playing organ music. "Hey

now," said the pilot. The ship somersaulted and descended. The radio stopped and the cruiser crashed in City Hall Plaza, some seven yards from an office building marked Police.

Bill hesitated on the curb in front of the hotel he was staying at. Finally he flagged an automatic taxi. The ground car stopped in front of him and he got in, giving Dr. Deeping's address.

He sat stiffly during the trip.

But the taxi arrived without any trouble.

12

Joker for Hire

Something came crunching across the simulated beach and then Daniel Godfrey's shoulder was poked by a shoed foot. He opened his eyes and looked up. His sweetheart was standing over him, fully clothed, a bundle of colored punch-cards in her slender hands. "Hello," said Dan, pushing himself up to a sitting position with his elbows.

"I thought you'd be here, Daniel," said Karen Singletree. "I've made up my mind. That's why I'm willing to give up my lunch period for you. Get dressed now, please."

Removing the tinted lenses from his eyeballs Dan said, "No job interviews today, Karen."

"Up, up," the pretty brunette said. She put all the cards in her left hand and knifed her flat right into the crotch at his shoulder joint. "It's all arranged."

Dan stood up and watched the blue ceiling of the indoor beach. Right on time the automated seagulls started to circle. "Karen, our agreement is I don't have to look for work on the day I pick up my unemployment check."

"Daniel," said Karen, "it's been three weeks since you were let go from the Prelim Processing Division of Suburban Clerical. Three weeks, Daniel. The grass is growing. The wheels are turning. And you? You're sitting on this beach with a lot of other ne'er-do-wells and freeloaders."

"And playboys," said Dan, finding his locker key under his towel. "Anyway, there hasn't been any grass in Keystone City for seventy years."

"A truism doesn't have to be technically accurate," the girl said. "Quick now. Get yourself all nice and presentable."

Dan rolled up his towel. "Where am I going?"

Karen smiled and held up the punchcards. "I had new copies made of all your records and résumés. My treat."

"Who am I talking to?"

The girl caught his shoulder and started him off toward the dressing rooms, which were disguised as native huts this week. "I wangled you a chance at the Vocational Lottery."

Dan stopped dead still. "No." He shook his head. "No, no, Karen. Just because I can't seem to hold a job for more than two or three months. No. I'm only twenty-seven after all. There's still hope."

"But," said Karen, lowering her voice, "will there be hope for us?"

"What?"

"You're turning into a beachcomber," the girl said. "Living off the state. Fight, Daniel. Please, fight."

"Who'll I fight?"

"I mean, fight for a place in Society."

"How's the Vocational Lottery going to help with that?" he asked. "It's all just a matter of chance with them."

"The girl in my building who shares my dispoze hole's husband won a vice presidency there. And he won't be twenty-five until autumn."

"Look," said Dan, "it's a fine gimmick for the government. In order to get people to volunteer for all the lousy jobs in this planet system they run the Vocational Lottery. They toss in a few soft jobs as bait. The rest of the jobs available are godawful, Karen. And isn't one of the rules that you have to work at whatever job you win for no less than six months?"

"Yes," she said. "That would be a record for you. No matter what the job." She made one hand into an encouraging fist. "I know you'll win a splendid job, Daniel."

"The odds are against my winning anything very good."

"Well," said Karen, "it's either the Lottery. Or goodbye."

Dan looked at her for a moment in the bright synthetic sunlight. "Okay, it's the Lottery."

The beaded curtain at the door of the Personnel Manager's office clicked and rattled a long time after Dan had entered and taken a purple interviewee chair.

The Personnel Manager of the Vocational Lottery was a thin, taut-skinned man of sixty. He wore formal attire and in his left eye there was an oversize, rose-tinted contact lens. "Your records seem to be all in order," he said, shuffling the punchcards into a neat pack.

"Thank you," said Dan.

"You've held quite a few jobs."

"I've never seemed to hit on the right one. I've got the idea that my guidance android in college was on the fritz. You really can't trust an android 100 percent, meaning no offense."

The manager stiffened. "I'm not an andy."

"I know," said Dan. "I just meant the whole Vocational Lottery seems to be staffed quite heavily with androids."

"Equal opportunity for all is our motto at the casino." The brittle old man rose, saying, "You understand the rules. We place your résumé card in a glass bowl and you wait until it is drawn by one of our staff of blindfolded little girls. Around the room in which the drawing is held are thirteen doors—I hope you aren't superstitious? No? Fine— At any one time only two of these doors will be unlocked. The open sequence changes as each card is drawn. When your name is called you start trying the doors. You must go through the first one that opens. You understand thus far?"

"Sure," said Dan. "Seems fair enough."

"Behind the door you will meet one of our Job Counselors. He will be, I'm afraid, an android."

"That's okay."

"Good. On his desk the Job Counselor will have three aruba shells."

"Beg pardon?"

"Aruba shells," said the Manager. "You know, the shell of an aruba."

"Oh, sure."

"You will be allowed to pick one shell. The Job Counselor will lift it and beneath you will find your job assignment."

"And if I don't like it?"

The old man smiled. "You have one escape clause. The Counselor is authorized to provide you with two bite-size capsules of poison. Otherwise, you must take the job. It's in the agreement you signed."

"My girl friend, Karen Singletree, signed that for me, I guess."

"You wish to reconsider?"

"No," said Dan. "People are always making decisions for me. No reason to stop now."

"That's the way." He put his hand on Dan's shoulder and led him down a softlit, thick-carpeted corridor.

"People really fit into the jobs they get this way?" Dan asked as he neared the swinging doors of the Lottery's Drawing Room.

"This system seems to work as well as any," the Personnel Manager said, sending Dan through the doors.

There was no one else on the flight to Murdstone. That was not surprising. Murdstone was the least favored planet in the drab Barnum system of planets. And right now it was having some kind of civil war or other. Daniel Godfrey wasn't too sure on the details. Karen had become hysterical halfway through her outlining of the political setup on Murdstone.

People always ended up blaming you for the results and consequences of the decisions they'd made for you. Karen didn't come to the spaceport to see Dan off. She had sent him an odd-shaped package. The package turned out to contain all his records and twenty-three copies of his résumé, topped off by their friendship ring.

Dan folded his arms and hunched down in the cracked pseudoplastic passenger chair. Karen had been counting on his coming out the Vocational Lottery with a good-paying executive job in some impressive and respectable industry.

The idea that Dan was going to Murdstone to be a Court Jester, though. That was too much for Karen to adjust to.

Even Dan was a little unsettled. He had no idea what the Monarchy of The Prime Territory was like or what they would find funny. Vocational Lottery had guaranteed on-the-job training.

He sank further into the seat and closed his eyes. No use worrying about it. For the next six months, no matter what, he'd have a steady job and he would not have to make a single decision. The situation had that to say for it.

A dust storm was sweeping across the rutted overgrown field of the spaceport. Three scarlet-uniformed musical androids went cartwheeling across the field, pushed by the wind.

"There goes the reception," said the silver-hatted young man who pulled Dan through a door marked Customs. "We'd planned on a few welcoming songs but the wind billowed away our band." He held out his hand. "My name is

Enforcer JG Buttoney. Sent out from the Palace at Prime Territory to greet you."

"Are you Customs, too?" asked Dan. The pilot had helped him carry his four pieces of luggage into this creaking building. They were sitting in a row between Dan and Buttoney.

"Thanks for reminding me," said Enforcer JG Buttoney, fishing a sticker out of an inside pocket. "Would you mind licking that? I have a thing about glue."

"Sure," said Dan. He ran his tongue along the sticker. "Now?"

"Oh, yes. Stick it on one of your bags. That should serve to make it all official." Buttoney smiled. "Off the cuff, I can tell you that this is not the height of the tourist season. Our Customs Inspector asked if he could take some time off to visit a second cousin of his in Territory #11."

"So you let him."

"No," said Buttoney, "we shot him. You don't ask for favors on Murdstone. We're under Royal Law right now, you know."

"I don't follow the news too closely."

"You wouldn't see it anyway," said the Junior Grade Enforcer. "We suppress all the news. Lot simpler than censoring every damn item that comes along." He glanced across the shadowy room. The wind outside was fading some and the harsh grating of the dust on the thin walls was subsiding. Near an empty, sprung-doored soft drink dispenser stood a short fat man in a loose blue suit. He had his hands in his pockets and seemed to be trying to outstare the brim of his yellow hat. Buttoney called to him. "Tomlin. Over here."

The fat man moved. He tipped his hat. He hitched up his pants. He came running toward them. Halfway there his foot seemed to catch in the cuff of his pants and he fell. He spun over twice and then slid on his back. He came to his feet a yard in front of Buttoney and Dan. "Yes, sir?"

The Enforcer JG took off his black-visored silver cap and bent forward. He laughed. He slapped his cap against the gold stripe on his trousers. "Beautiful," he said. "That is a classic."

Tomlin curtsied. "Yes, sir."

"Seriously," said Buttoney, catching his breath. "Give Daniel Godfrey here a hand with his luggage. Stow it in the halftrack."

The fat man picked up the two heaviest pieces and shuffled off. "Yes, sir."

Buttoney looked after him, shaking his head. "Splendid. Really classic, wasn't it?"

"His falling down?" said Dan, catching hold of the remaining suitcases.

"I suppose it's not as funny to you as it is to me. You being in the business. I think, though, that you're going to find Tomlin an excellent assistant."

"Oh, so?" said Dan. "My assistant?"

"Right. Tomlin is Assistant Court Jester. He has a really classic approach to the comedic art. Boy."

Approaching the halftrack parked down from the spaceport building Dan got control of himself. If they wanted him to fall down, he'd fall down. He was obliging. Besides which, he was stuck here on Murdstone for six months.

There was a girl standing alongside Tomlin. A tall slender girl with her dark orange scarf wrapped around her face against the dust.

"The press," said Buttoney into Dan's ear.

"I thought you'd stamped it out."

"We still let the folks at home read a little something. Sports, propaganda, show biz doings and social notes. That girl is Jean Parchman of the *Prime Territory News-Flame*. Cute kid."

"She here to cover my arrival?"

"It's show biz news. Yes."

They reached the halftrack. The storm was dying, the dust was swirling sluggishly. Dan put his suitcases where

Tomlin indicated and then took the back seat Buttoney pointed at.

The newspaper girl got in the truck and took the seat beside him. She unwound the scarf. "I'm Jean Parchman of the *News-Flame*. I understand you're the new Chief Court Jester."

Dan started to answer.

From the front seat Buttoney said, "I'm taping all this, Jean honey. Okay?"

"Certainly. That's the law." She had light blonde hair and a pretty, faintly freckled face.

"Yes, I'm the new jester," Dan said.

Tomlin started the truck and they turned out onto the narrow highway that led in lazy arcs through the dry fields that surrounded the spaceport.

"My uncle helped design this Super Roadway," said Buttoney over his shoulder.

"It has a nice shape to it," Dan said.

"Your name is?" asked the girl.

"Daniel Godfrey. From the planet Barnum."

"How long have you been in the entertainment line?"

Dan said, "I've always had an interest in the performing arts."

"Jean honey," said the JG Enforcer, "I'll give you the bio throwaway that the Senior Informer's Office has made up on Dan. You can skip that part of it, huh?"

"Certainly," said the girl reporter, smiling at the back of Buttoney's head. "What's your favorite vegetable?"

Dan hesitated, waiting for Buttoney to turn again. Dan said finally, "Squash."

"Favorite color?"

"Blue."

"How old are you?"

"Twenty-seven."

The girl sighed and relaxed. She crossed her legs and hooked her folded hands over her knee. "I think that takes care of it."

Dan asked, "You don't take notes?"

"No," said Jean. "Enforcer Buttoney will just give me a transcript of his bugtape. Lots easier."

Fields passed and houses appeared. The road circled in and out between them. The few people who were outside seemed to drift inside as the official car approached.

The houses were small, thin walled. With mud roofs and opaque windows. "The slums?" said Dan.

The girl elbowed him gently. "One of the suburbs of Prime Territory's Capital City."

"Compact housing is the order of the day on Murdstone," explained Enforcer JG Buttoney.

They traveled for nearly twenty miles and neither the houses nor the people changed. The only variety was afforded by the occasional movements of groups of white-uniformed men among the houses.

"Police?" Dan asked Jean.

"No," she said. "Enquirers."

"Which means?"

"We have," said Buttoney, talking across his resting elbow, "periodic quizzes."

"To give prizes?"

"To determine who'll be shot each day," said Buttoney.

"There's a public shooting twice a day," said Jean, turning to look out the window.

"We get some swell turnouts for the executions. It's entertaining and it keeps the lowers in place."

"Murdstone," said the girl, "is a two-class planet. In each of our territories there are two classes. The lowers and the ruling."

"I don't know much about politics," said Dan.

The truck was pulling now as the road began to climb through gradual hills. There were no houses anymore. Slowly all around a forest appeared. Tall green leafed trees, stretching away in neat rows, long strips of cool shadow between them. Up here there was no dust storm.

"No housing within a mile of the Capital," said Jean.

Dan nodded. To make conversation he said to the girl, "And what's your favorite food, Miss Parchman?"

She glanced at him, smiling. "MPF."

Dan frowned. "MPF?"

"Multi Purpose Food," said Buttoney. "The lowers eat that exclusively."

"You're . . ."

"Lower," said the girl. "But since I work on the paper I'm allowed to live within the walls. Quite a few lowers are for various reasons."

"Darn good little reporter," said Buttoney.

In front of them on the road now was a wall fifty feet high. It was grey in color and made of some glistening pock-surfaced material. No opening appeared in the wall.

"Excuse me," said Enforcer JG Buttoney as the truck stopped some dozen yards from the big wall. "I'll trot up and identify us." He left the halftrack and walked with his hands over his head, stopping flat against the wall. Buttoney muttered something and a small slit opened in the wall at eye level.

"They have his retinal pattern on file," said Jean.

"I thought so," said Dan.

Tomlin turned his head and winked at Dan. "Some fun, isn't it?"

Dan didn't answer.

They rehearsed outdoors. In a square of dull yellow grass behind one of the garage areas. From here you saw the backside of the palace, high blank walls and towers.

"Timing is everything," said Tomlin, selecting a new tomato from the basket that rested near his feet. "This time don't flinch. When I grind it into your face don't react right away. See? Count up to three, slow. Then you casually reach inside your coat and get the eggs. Got it?"

Dan had on a loose suit, similar in style to Tomlin's. His

hat was different and had a removable brim for comedy purposes. "When do you think we'll go on?"

Tomlin lifted his head and looked at the blank walls behind them. He patted his right hand three times on the flat of his hat. After a few seconds he said, "Friend of mine on monitoring today. He'll aim the pickup gun away for awhile and we can talk without being recorded."

"They record us?" asked Dan. "All the time?"

"For the files of the Enforcers and Enquirers. Now then. What do you know about the setup here on Murdstone?"

"I haven't," said Dan, "learned much in the two days I've been here. I read the *News-Flame* every morning. Mostly for Miss Parchman's column. There's not much news in it."

"Okay," said Tomlin, putting his hand on Dan's arm. "Listen. The whole planet is ruled here from Prime Territory. Commander Brix is in charge of The Board of Rulers."

"I saw a poem about him on the front page of the paper."

"The Poet Laureate has a daily feature about old Brix. The thing I want you to understand is this. The government is pretty shaky. There's a guy named Felix Quarrie. A rebel, with a growing guerrilla army. He hangs out in the undeveloped areas of Murdstone, of which there are a lot. Quarrie you won't read about in the paper. They pretend he does not exist. All the tightening of rules, though, is to try and stamp out the guerrillas. What kind of mood do you think this puts Commander Brix in?"

"A lousy one."

"Right. Do you know where the last Court Jester went?" Dan blinked. "To a better job?"

"He was the morning execution three weeks ago."

"Great fringe benefit that is," said Dan. "That's great. How'd he work that?"

"Brix wasn't amused. You see, they have us come in and try to cheer them all up at banquets and board meetings. Bastian, your predecessor, didn't go over too good at a pretty gloomy board meeting. So, no more Bastian."

Dan sat down on the grass. "Swell. Great. And when is it we go on?"

Tomlin shrugged. "They're in so foul a mood they apparently don't even want to see us. There are some serious meetings going on." He took a couple more tomatoes from the basket and started juggling them. "No jokes about guerrillas or rebels. Try to make everybody laugh. That's my advice to you." He tossed the tomatoes into Dan's lap and gave his unseen friend the signal to start recording again.

A chill draft seemed to be circling the alcove just beyond the board meeting chambers. Dan tried pacing but he kept getting tangled in his baggy pants. He stopped and checked over again the ripe fruit and vegetables that Tomlin had laid out on the wooden benches against the wall.

Tomlin came silently in the back way with some plyofilm bladders filled with ink and glue. "Sure fire stuff," he said, making room for them next to a still life of tomatoes and bananas.

Dan nodded and moved up to the thick curtain that masked the alcove. There was an eye-size spy hole in the curtain so that jesters might watch the meeting room and come in on cue. The wide round meeting room was hung with scarlet draperies. In its center was a vast rectangular table with a dozen heavy chairs around it. None of the board members had arrived yet.

For two weeks now Dan had been working up an act with Tomlin. The first summons to perform had come this morning. Dan was uncertain. But Tomlin assured him their new routines were sure fire. He jumped when Tomlin touched his shoulder. "What?"

The fat assistant clown handed him an earplug speaker. Tomlin inserted one in his own ear and said, "They should be shuffling in soon. This is to let you know what's being said."

Twisting in the tiny speaker, Dan went back to watching

the board room. The far doors whipped open and an old man in a fur-trimmed jade green uniform came in. Two green-uniformed men of lesser rank helped him by the elbows.

Tomlin took a look. "Counselor Mather," he said toward Dan's free ear. "In charge of Child Welfare."

Mather was put in a chair halfway down the table. As soon as his aides let go his arms he whacked one of them with his gold-tassled riding crop. "Must not squeeze so hard next time."

Eventually eleven chairs were filled with Counselors, Enforcers and Enquirers.

Tomlin unscrewed his ear speaker and held it out from his head. "Should be time for Commander Brix to appear."

Dan squinted, his eye touching the curtain. The entrance doors were held wide by two broad-shouldered guards. Then six trumpeteers dived into the room. The blast made Dan jump back. When his head cleared he looked again. The board members were standing. At the table's head was a small old man, covered with white and gold. He wore a short jacketed uniform with gold trim, gold medals and gold buttons. From his gold crash helmet fluttered a fan-like white plume. On his right side hung a gold blaster pistol and on his left a gold sword. His face was walnut-like and his white eyebrows made a thick straight line over his small eyes. All the wrinkles of his face pointed downward. The Commander coughed once and put his fingers carefully against his mouth. "Well, boys, let's get cracking."

Dan wandered away from the peephole and strolled by the fruit and vegetables.

"This propaganda thing," Commander Brix was saying, "has got my goat. These silly guerrillas are making points with the lowers. How are we going to quash it?"

"Well," said someone, "here's my thinking on it. Let's step up the shootings."

"Wait, wait," said another voice. "Let me hitchhike on

that idea if I may. How about instead of just the same old run of the mill firing squads we introduce a hangman or two? Maybe even a head-chopper if the budget allows."

"Budget isn't the problem. I think we should go for saturation on the shooting angle. Step up the executions per day."

"But how do people really feel about shooting? I'm asking because frankly I am not sure. Couldn't we run a check? That would be the way to really find out for sure. See if hanging or decapitating would go over as well."

"Flogging," cried Counselor Mather. "When we had good old-fashioned flogging there wasn't half the sassiness there is now."

"What say we run a test on it? Out in Territory #14 we start hanging them and in #20, say, to name a territory at random, we set up a chopping block. It would not hurt to try it for a few weeks."

"Flog the whole sassy bunch!"

The meeting continued. Five and a half hours later it was agreed to give other means of execution a trial run and determine how effective they were in keeping the increasingly restless lowers in check. After considerable debate it was agreed to try a week of flogging out in Territory #23. Counselor Mather also proposed a reward of 100,000 credits to anyone who would get hold of the rebel leader, Felix Quarrie, and thrash him. Then there was some discussion as to the differences and similarities between thrashing and flogging.

Dan and Tomlin ate a few of the props and waited. Nearly seven hours from the starting time of the meeting Commander Brix announced, "My stomach's growling. Let's call it a day."

"How about some jesters to cheer us up?" asked Counselor Mather, slapping something with his riding crop.

"Raincheck that," said Brix. "I'm too frazzled to laugh. Tomorrow maybe."

The meeting adjourned and soon the big room was cold and silent.

"There's a fine line with ripe vegetables," said Tomlin, starting to gather up their equipment. "Some of this may be spoiled before tomorrow."

"That's it?" said Dan, at the curtain. "We don't go on at all?"

"It works out like that now and then," said Tomlin. "These are troubled times."

"That they are," said Dan, taking the speaker from his ear.

The next morning, before the heat came on, two Enquirers broke into Dan's room.

"Ooops," said Dan, sitting up in his cot and blinking at the broken door. "It was open."

"We always like to break in," said the heavier of the two men. A dark moustached fellow with rosy cheeks. "We picked that up from a Psychological Warfare course. I'm Enquirer JG Weldon."

"I'm Enquirer JG Brinker," said the other. He had a flat pale face.

Dan swung his feet to the floor. The floor and the scatter rug were cold. "Something you wanted?" Yesterday's summons to perform hadn't taken this shape.

Weldon frowned around at the small sparse room. "We'll have to take him over to an Interrogation Suite maybe, Charles."

"Looks as though, Bryan."

"Book a nice big room at the Enquiry Arms Hotel."

"One sec," said Enquirer JG Brinker. "Perhaps the angle I suggested will pay off and the suite won't be called into play."

Weldon cocked his head. "That's a thought."

Dan put on his robe. "What exactly is going on?"

Brinker took something out of his uniform jacket. "What do you think this is?"

It seemed to be several sheets of folded paper. "Some sheets of folded paper?"

"Is that really what you think?"

"Or it could be letters or notes. I don't know."

"You see?" Brinker asked Weldon.

"A put-on maybe," replied Weldon.

"Here, look," he said, handing the stuff to Dan.

It was a pamphlet. Printed hastily on cheap grade paper. "It's a book, huh?"

"A book*let*," said Brinker. "You haven't paid enough attention to the title."

The pamphlet's face said: Even A Fool Can See; being a Report on the Injustices of Murdstone, and written by a dull-witted person, who never-the-less can Perceive the Numerous Faults of Commander Brix. A Political Essay by Daniel Godfrey, Court Jester.

Dan slowly held the booklet out from him. "Well."

"Did you write that?" asked Weldon.

"No."

Brinker smiled at his partner. "We've checked your movements thoroughly, Daniel. A real sifting job. We can't see how you could have an opportunity to slip out and have that printed." He didn't take the pamphlet back from Dan.

Finally Dan set the thing down on the bed. "I don't quite get this."

"It's Charles' theory that whoever wrote the booklet simply took your name to use as a symbol."

"I'm a symbol already and I haven't even performed?"

"The show biz sections of the papers gave you quite a lot of space," said Brinker. "Often the name of the Court Jester in Prime Territory is used by the lowers as a synonym for a dull stupid person. Until now there has been no propaganda use of such a name, however."

"Fine," said Dan, sitting down on his cot alongside the pamphlet.

"You seem not to be involved in this," said Brinker. "For now, since you are a newcomer, we'll let it ride."

"Let's go, Charles," said Weldon, "before that waitress I'm fond of in the gruel line goes off duty."

The two JG Enquirers said goodbye and left.

By midday Dan got the JG Royal Carpenters to put up a new door on his room. He closed the door and sat down in his chair. He took up the pamphlet and started reading it.

Something about it was faintly familiar. As he read, he found himself agreeing with this Daniel Godfrey. When he finished Dan stood up, anxious to go out and start something.

There was nowhere he could go and nothing he could do. He realized that and sat down. He hoped nobody would make any more trouble for him.

Three days later another pamphlet with the Daniel Godfrey byline appeared and the Enforcers and Enquirers moved Dan into an Interrogation Suite. The room was twice as large as his old one at the Palace.

Enquirer JG Weldon dropped in fairly often. "Wouldn't you like to confess?" he was asking again now.

Dan said, "I want to cooperate. The thing is, I didn't write those booklets."

"I'm at sixes and sevens," admitted Weldon. "None of the truth serums got any results."

"That last one made a red spot," said Dan, tapping his arm.

"Our Inquisitor Androids drew a blank."

"Is that big silver-plated one going to be okay?"

"Yes, he just needs a new generator." Weldon scratched at his moustache. "Even the torture didn't get any answers out of you."

Dan turned away from the JG Enforcerer, not saying anything.

"Did we hurt your feelings?" asked Weldon. "I myself wanted to skip the torture. But old Counselor Mather kept agitating for torture."

Dan nodded. "I figure that's why I was flogged."

Weldon's rosy cheeks grew flushed. "We're all afraid of a revolt, you see. Most of us are hoping against hope that you really are the one who authored all this inflammatory propaganda. Then we'd be able to do something about it. We don't have any other leads."

"That's too bad," said Dan.

"Counselor Mather has suggested," said Weldon, "that we execute you as a gesture. It might make a nice spectacle for the people. Should you somehow be the one who is writing the terrible booklets we'd also put a stop to them."

"Since I'm not, the booklets will keep coming out after you do me in. That would give a mystical touch to the whole business."

"I pointed that out to old Mather. He agreed to settle for a public flogging come this weekend."

Carefully Dan sat down. "I hope I'll be recovered from the last flogging by then."

"We can always postpone a day or so. Not too long, mind you. The lowers are really getting violent." Weldon smiled. "If you should decide to confess don't hesitate to call me at any time. Best take it easy for the rest of today. Get in shape for the big flogging."

Weldon went away. Dan rested tentatively in his chair. They'd left him copies of the second pamphlet to refresh his memory. Dan got one and read it again.

Daniel Godfrey was even better in this one. There was a very well-written and moving attack on Commander Brix and the whole Murdstone government. A step-by-step program for overthrow was included, too.

After Dan had gone over both pamphlets several times he took up the afternoon edition of the *News-Flame* and skimmed through it. He slowed down for Jean Parchman's column. That he always read in full. The girl turned out a good column, always well-written and moving.

Dan folded up the paper. That's why the style of the booklets seemed somehow familiar. Not because he'd written them himself in some kind of trance. But because they were written in a style that echoed subtly Jean Parchman's.

Now here was a problem. If he told them his suspicions he might be able to clear himself. Or he could keep quiet and ride the interrogation out. It would mean, at the least, one more beating.

Still, though, from the little he'd seen and heard of Murdstone he agreed with what the girl said in the pamphlets. And Jean Parchman was good-looking, too.

Dan decided. He would keep quiet.

The flogging was called off. The third Daniel Godfrey booklet had been widely distributed in all the territories and it had produced, once read, a general revolt.

This caused Commander Brix himself to visit Dan. His gold helmet had a dent in it and the white plume was askew. "An assassination attempt while I was opening a new MPF cafeteria downtown," the Commander said, seating himself in Dan's chair and putting the hat on his knee. "You still work for us, you know, Daniel."

"Yes, sir."

"Here's what we've decided. It's a desperate measure but we think you'll comply."

"I get executed, huh?"

"On the contrary. You address a rally in the Palace Bowl. So far the citizens in the Prime Territory area have remained loyal. We intend to let in five thousand of them, hand-picked, to hear your Bowl talk. The talk will also be broadcast to all territories."

"You think a comedy routine will stop the revolution?"

"No," said Brix. "We're going to beat the enemy at its own dodge. You, Daniel, will get up and admit that you indeed are the Daniel Godfrey who wrote the pamphlets. However, you will laugh at the things. Explain that it was a prank. A merry jest."

"That'll work?"

"Propaganda started it, propaganda will stop it. You say it was all a joke. No conspiracy can stand laughter. The fangs will be removed by this little maneuver. Your speech is being written now. You'll speak tomorrow at sunset."

"So soon?"

"These are troubled times."

"I know, I know."

The five thousand people in the torch-lit audience could not see him yet. From the left stage entrance to the open-air theater Dan had watched as the semi-circles of stone seats filled up. Across the empty stage Commander Brix glittered, waiting to go on.

Someone touched Dan's arm.

"Any statement for the press?" Jean Parchman asked.

There was, at the moment, no one around them. Enquirer JG Weldon and Enforcer JG Buttoney were still down in the dressing rooms putting on their makeup. The Enforcer Cadets who had led Dan up to the wings had drifted back a few yards.

"Listen, Miss Parchman," he said.

"Call me, Jean, Dan."

"I'll call you Daniel Godfrey if it's okay."

The girl smiled. "We'll talk that over later. They'll kill you after you make this speech, you know." Her head angled slightly in the direction of the Enforcer Cadets. "They're with us. I've come to get you out."

"You have, huh?"

"Yes, it's all been decided."

The Commander stepped warily out on the stage and the Prime Territory Anthem was played. Armed Enforcer Cadets were scattered in the orchestra pit and in the aisles.

"Come on," Jean said, catching at Dan's arm.

"No," Dan said, "I've gotten in enough grief with letting people decide things for me."

"You're dead if you don't come."

"One thing," Dan said as the music stopped and the Commander started his introduction. "Are there any good beaches around here? Real ones, I mean."

"Yes."

"Wait here," Dan said. "I'll be back shortly."

Fortunately Commander Brix said little more than, "Here is a fine young man to explain things to you. I give you Murdstone's favorite new author and humorist, Daniel Godfrey."

Dan stepped onto the stone stage and walked up to the Commander's side. There was considerable applause and shouting.

"It's all a joke," Brix whispered to him. "Stress that. Add to the script if you like. But get that across." He moved off into the wings.

Dan adjusted the microphone and waited for quiet. Then he said, "Please don't applaud until I finish, ladies and gentlemen. This is a proud moment for me. The government has asked me to announce its resignation. Henceforward I am to be titular ruler of Murdstone, until such time as popular elections can be held. I thank you."

Commander Brix and Counselor Mather tried to get at Dan with gold-tasseled riding crops but the audience was coming up on the stage now and the Commander and Mather got carried off into the darkness beyond the torchlight. The armed Enforcers had hesitated when they'd heard what Dan said. The ones who hadn't decided to join the crowd had been disarmed before anyone could give a counter order.

Dan managed to get backstage to Jean Parchman. "I thought it would be quicker this way."

"How can we know you're any better than Brix?" The girl was pale, shaking.

"You can't right now. You should have considered that before you used my name."

"That just came to me as a gimmick. Once I had the

gimmick the stuff all fell into place," the girl said. "Because you're supposed to be a fool."

"How soon can you get Felix Quarrie here?"

"So you can execute him?"

"No more executions. I want to talk to him."

"A day or two."

The citizens of Prime Territory located Dan and carried him around on their shoulders until long after all the torches had gone out.

There was no pattern to the seagulls' flight. The sand was soft and the sky a warm blue.

Dan folded his copy of the new *News-Flame* on his chest and closed his eyes.

A bare toe nudged his shoulder. "Dan."

He sat up. "Jean."

She spread her towel out next to his. "Mind?"

"No."

"Elections will be next month."

"Good idea."

"You're really serious about this?"

"That's why I made Felix Quarrie temporary President of Murdstone," Dan said. "See, I finally decided. The best times I've had have been between jobs. I'm not cut out for Data Processing or Android Supplementing or Pre-Clerical or Court Jestering. I just like to hang around the beaches."

"You don't want to run Murdstone?"

"No. I'm not cut out for that either." He grinned at the girl. "That's why I took advantage of my position here. And granted myself lifetime unemployment insurance. My last official act."

The girl shook her head. "It's not that bad an idea, I guess."

"Let me buy you a soft drink or something?"

Jean said, "No thanks, Dan. I'm in a real rush. I can only stay a few minutes."

Dan nodded and stretched out again. He closed his eyes.

13

Terminal

It was while the tacky white-enameled android was putting the second scoop of beans on his breakfast tray that Penrose began to wonder if he was really old. Penrose put one hand flat on his face, feeling for wrinkles. The serving android slipped another scoop of beans out of the cauldron set in its chest. This one missed the tray and dropped on to the tan blanket of Penrose's bed. The android ticked and more beans fell on the cot.

The old man in the next bed stretched a foot out from under the covers and kicked the andy. The machine ratcheted and whirred, then said, "Good morning. Have a happy day." It rolled away to serve the fat man across the aisle.

"I'm Harrison," said the old man who had booted the android. He was lanky, weathered. His face had deep sharp wrinkles. He turned slightly in the bunk and Penrose saw that he had only one arm.

Penrose hesitated. "I'm Penrose," he said finally. "Excuse me. I'm fuzzy about things." He couldn't remember even yesterday, he realized now.

Harrison swallowed a spoonful of orange beans. "You know where you are, don't you?"

Their room was small, metallic, with a low gray ceiling. There were six beds in it. Only five of them occupied. At the far end was a red metal door. "I guess," said Penrose. "I'm not certain."

"Where do you think?"

Penrose looked down at his tray. The two scoops of beans had collapsed into a single pool. "Well, this is Greater Los Angeles. And the date is . . . it's October 15, 2046. Yes. I know that."

"It's the 16th," corrected Harrison.

Nodding, Penrose said, "Oh, that's right. I'm missing a day."

"You're in Senior Citizens' Terminal #130," said Harrison.

The men in the other beds were old, too, like Harrison. Penrose touched his face again. "I'm not quite sure why I'm here. I've been having trouble remembering exactly. I have a feeling I'm not . . . not a senior citizen."

"Neither am I," called the fat old man across the aisle. He was pink and grey.

"That's Carlisle," said Harrison. "He has memory trouble, too."

"I know you, Harrison," said Carlisle. "You're a mean old coot. You're old enough to be my grandfather. You maybe are my grandfather. He was a mean old one-armed man, too. Except it was his right arm he was lacking."

The serving android was making harsh scraping sounds now. It had stopped by the bed of a small quiet old man. The man was flat on his back, not moving, breathing softly through his mouth. His hair was long and fine and his skin was a transparent blue-white. "Good morning. Have a happy day," said the android, propping the old man up and spoon feeding him from the cauldron.

"That's Guttenberg," said Harrison. "He's eighty."

"I bet he doesn't know who he is either," said Carlisle.

Penrose watched Harrison finish breakfast. "Is everyone sick here?"

"No," said Harrison. "You must know all about the Senior Citizens' Terminals. Think about it."

Penrose leaned back against the metal head rest. "The Senior Citizens' Terminals," he said, "are under the juris-diction of the United States Welfare Squad. And are free to all. The problem of the aged is at a stage of solution never before known. Nearly one hundred old timers are collected each month in each terminal. Because of the Welfare Squad these old folks can live out their golden days without fear of burdening their friends and relations." Now that he thought about it Penrose realized he knew a lot about the terminals. But he didn't know why he was here.

"You're doing excellently," said old Harrison. "Do you recall the recruiting part of this setup?"

"Stop now," said Carlisle. "I'm trying to recollect who I really am and your talk is unsettling to me."

"You're Carlisle," said Harrison. "A retired data processor."

"No, I'm not," said the heavy old man. "I'm a spry young fellow with a name that starts with W."

"About recruiting," Harrison said to Penrose.

Penrose concentrated. "It is the function of the Welfare Squad to recruit at least a minimum quota of old folks each collection period. Those old timers who are not reclaimed in thirty days are then processed at no extra cost."

"Quit," called out Carlisle. "I don't want to hear about that."

"He's been here twenty-eight days," said Harrison.

The fifth man in the room stood up on top of his cot. He was small with straight-standing white hair and black pockets under his pale eyes.

"There are things of which I may not speak;
There are thoughts that make the strong heart weak,
And bring a pallor to the cheek,
And a mist before the eye,"

he said.

"That's Remmeroy," said Harrison. "He gets processed next week."

Remmeroy's bed was suddenly pulled out from under him and slid back into the gray metal wall. The old man thunked to the floor.

Harrison swung out of his cot just as it shot away and he caught Penrose up and out of his. "We arise abruptly in this place."

The serving android opened a panel in the wall and buzzed out of the room. "Have a happy day."

The big blond recreational android jobbled Penrose by the shoulder. "No wool gathering, Fowler. This is letter writing time."

Penrose had almost remembered something important "I'm not Fowler," he said.

The second joggle was harsher. "Letter writing time, pops."

"Sorry," he said. He picked up the speaker tube of the lap letteriter. The andy moved on and Penrose dictated, "To whom it may concern. I still don't know what I'm doing here. I am confused and depressed."

The letteriter jumped out of his lap and began bouncing on the floor, making a bleeting sound. "Negative, negative."

The blond andy was at his shoulder again. "Fowler, you're not doing so good today."

"I guess not."

"You *guess*? Gramps, you *know* not. Now I want you to speak a nice pleasant letter. Get me?"

"Yes, sir." The letteriter crawled up his left leg and settled into his lap, nudging him sharply in the groin. "I'm not sure," said Penrose, "who it is I'm writing to."

"The therapy," said the blond android, "is in the act and is not involved with the recipient at all."

"Hello, everybody," dictated Penrose. "I'm having a great time here." He felt the android's grip lessen. "I'm having a happy day." The hand was lifted away but Penrose kept saying cheerful things.

Carlisle was having trouble. "I'm trying to communicate with my girl friend," he told the rec andy. "Her name begins with an F or an S."

"Just say you're fond of her," answered the android.

"I am, I am," said Carlisle. "I can't start off the letter with 'Dear F or S.' You see?"

"Start."

"Sweetheart," said Carlisle into his tube.

Remmeroy used his letteriter standing up. He was hunched in a corner with it under his arm.

> "When the lamp is shattered
> The light in the dust lies dead—
> When the cloud is scattered,
> The rainbow's glory is shed.
> When the lute is broken,
> Sweet tunes are remembered not. . . ."

"That's right," said the passing android. "Keep it cheerful."

Guttenberg, his hands limp at his sides, was propped in a chair. "Come on, gramps," said the android. "Talk. Send off something friendly to your loved ones."

Penrose turned to Harrison, who was sitting next to him, his letter writing done. "Why don't they leave Guttenberg alone? He can't even speak, can he?"

"No," said Harrison.

"It doesn't make sense."

"Not efficient, is it?"

Penrose hesitated. "The Welfare Squad has an able and qualified staff of checkers, the Efficiency Detail. It is their duty to make a thorough inspection periodically of each and every Senior Citizens' Terminal."

"Yes, that's true," said Harrison.

"Of course," said Penrose, "fellows in the Efficiency Detail are overworked and underpaid. Sometimes they can't be as thorough as they'd like to be."

The recreational andy held the speaker up near Guttenberg's mouth. "A ten-word message, pops. You can do that much. Come on."

"Can't we stop him?" Penrose asked.

"He turns off automatically when the recreation period ends. Guttenberg is able to hold out till then."

"This happens every day?"

Harrison nodded.

"Therapy time," announced a crisp voice from the wall.

The blond android let go of Guttenberg.

The therapist was shaped like a portable safe and had a gun-metal finish.

"Now," said Penrose when it was his turn, "this is going to sound odd to you."

"Not at all, Mr. Fowler," said the metal box in a warm voice.

Penrose fidgeted on the armchair that had come up through the floor. "First off, I'm not Fowler. I'm Penrose. Now here's the situation as I see it. Let me, by the way, apologize for being vague in some of the details. I realize now that I've probably been given some kind of medication. Look," he said, rolling up the sleeve of his tan shirt, "you can't help but see the needle marks, several of them. And some in my backside, too. While I appreciate the smooth efficient way I was given medical aid I have to say I'm disturbed that I haven't snapped out of it better."

"Yes, of course, Mr. Fowler," said the therapist.

"No, I'm not Fowler. Let's skip that for a minute. I think I had some sort of accident or something and was taken maybe to the nearest hospital. Fine. However, there seems to be a mistake being made. I'm not this Fowler. In fact you can see that I'm not even old. I'm not a senior citizen. It's hardly efficient, is it? To keep me on here."

"Certainly, certainly."

"When I woke up this morning I was much fuzzier than I am now. Things are starting to fill in for me. I'm certain I'm about thirty-four years old. There must be, though I can't remember it as yet, some useful function I fill on the outside. Some part of the essential function of Greater Los Angeles."

"That's surely possible," answered the therapist.

"All you have to do is let them know at Central Control and I'll be able to take off. You must have my outside clothes and ID packet and money someplace."

"You realize that in a terminal of this size we cannot be responsible for loss of property," said the machine. "Theft of belongings is naturally lamentable. The responsibility cannot be assumed, however, by the terminal staff."

"No," said Penrose, "I'm not grousing about my belongings. Let's go back to the fact that I'm only thirty-four years old. I don't belong here."

"To be sure."

"Then you'll do something?"

"You can assume that your problem will be given all the attention it warrants," said the therapist. "I must be getting on to my next patient."

"When exactly will you let me know?" Penrose asked as the machine started to roll toward Carlisle's chair.

"Yes, yes," it said and began talking to Carlisle.

Penrose glanced hopefully at Harrison and the one-armed man smiled back.

After lunch came sitting. Not in the soft chairs that had appeared for therapy but in stiff straight metal ones.

Penrose had his hands capping his knees. "Essentially,"

he said to Harrison, "the terminals are a positive thing. A solution to the problem of senior clutter."

"That's the Welfare Squad point of view." Harrison's hand rested on his chest.

"Those old timers who don't function any more in the highly overstocked urban and suburban complex are weeded out," said Penrose. "Should it turn out that an individual senior citizen still has a valid function he can always be reclaimed."

"They say the actual termination is pleasant."

Looking at the red door Penrose said, "Right beyond there, isn't it?"

"Yes. This is one of the waiting rooms. You can spend from a day to a week or more here. Depends on processing."

After a moment Penrose said, "I should be back home by late today."

"You know about yourself?"

Penrose shook his head. "Not entirely. I'm aware that I'm only thirty-four. I'm in this terminal by mistake. All the details on myself haven't come back to me as yet."

"Still," said Harrison, "don't you wonder?"

"Wonder about what?"

"If this terminal has made a mistake. Perhaps others do, too. Perhaps this one has before."

"No," said Penrose, "that's why they have the Efficiency Detail."

"They slipped up in your case."

There was a brief confusion because Guttenberg fell over sideways out of his chair. Carlisle and Remmeroy righted him.

"A system like this has to have a human element," said Penrose. "Even though the terminal itself is fully automatic. The Efficiency Detail provides that human element. That's why I know the error in my case will be cleared up."

"Suppose," said Harrison.

Remmeroy hopped up on his chair.

> "I remember, I remember
> The house where I was born,
> The little window where the sun
> Came peeping in at morn."

"Suppose what?" asked Penrose.

Harrison shrugged his armless shoulder. "That an Efficiency Detail man came here to Terminal #130 to inspect. They work solo, you know."

"The budget doesn't allow for teams."

"Possibly the last time the Efficiency Detail man was through he overlooked a faulty rail on a ramp. This time as he leaned on it he fell and whacked his head. While he was unconscious, before the automatic staff rushed to help, someone might have switched papers with him. Someone named Fowler say. By the time the staff gave him treatment for his fall and shots this Efficiency Detail man would be pretty confused. The equipment here, a lot of it anyway, is old and erratic and they might easily get him mixed up with one of these old fellows. One on his way to a termination waiting room."

"Oh, that's very unlikely," said Penrose.

"I was a rich fuel speculator," said Carlisle. "Before I got mixed up with this wild bunch here. Youngest fellow in my profession. How about you?" he called out to Penrose.

"I can't," he said, "quite remember."

"Does it start with a W?"

The chairs retracted and it was time for naps, the wall told them.

Harrison frowned. "Penrose was with the Efficiency Detail."

Penrose was put to sleep before he could say anything to Harrison.

The serving android was backed into a corner.

"On the blink again," said Carlisle.

For dinner a table had appeared. The five men were arranged around it.

"I'll give it a kick," said Harrison.

Penrose jumped up and got to the android first. "Would you please get hold of the therapist for me."

"Happy day," said the machine.

"Look," said Penrose. "That Harrison. He's trying to tell me I've somehow been mistaken for an old man named Fowler. That it's this Fowler's turn to be terminated today. That kind of mistake is not going to look good on the records." He touched one sticky arm of the enameled android. "I don't know, Harrison could be lying. He says I'm with the Efficiency Detail. The drugs you people gave me. I'm still fuzzy. Will you tell the therapist to please, god, hurry. In case it is true."

"Choice of desert," the andy said.

Remmeroy ran around the table and came slowly toward Penrose and the android.

> "The sea is calm tonight,
> The tide is full, the moon lies fair."

The old man slammed his fist against the machine and broke his hand.

Penrose exhaled sharply. Somebody would have to come now and look after Remmeroy. Then he'd be able to get word out. If he were with the Efficiency Detail they wouldn't be missing him yet. He only had to report in once a week. He covered a good part of Greater Los Angeles and didn't have to file anything until the end of each work week.

Still the Efficiency Detail might be wondering about him already. He'd been here two days now apparently. He didn't recall a family. Civil servants didn't have time for close ties usually.

Remmeroy returned to the table. His good hand locked around his other wrist. He howled once and spun. Then sat quietly in his chair.

Nothing came to help him.

"The night nurse has some loose valves," said Harrison. "May not come at all tonight."

"I was the youngest real doctor in my home town," said Carlisle. "My home town began with a D or an S."

Penrose cupped his hands to his mouth and yelled.

The red door swung open and the lights in the gray room dimmed.

"Sorry," said Harrison, turning away.

Two bright silver androids rolled out of the room beyond the red door. They slid over the floor and took hold of Penrose.

"This is going to mean trouble," said Penrose.

Something jabbed his arm.

"Now, now," said one of the androids. It had the same voice as the therapist. "Things are okay."

"Perfectly," added the other.

They took him into the termination room and guided him into its one straight chair. The chair, once his weight hit it, extended restraining straps around him.

Penrose was not as clear as he had been. "Be sure my message gets through," he said.

The androids were gone and the door closed.

There was a wet sound now. A waterfall it sounded like. And soft organ music began to fill the room.

Penrose tried to remember. He couldn't quite believe that Harrison was right. That he was with the Welfare Squad, with the Efficiency Detail.

It didn't seem to him that he could have been a part of a setup like this. Not at all.

A silver tube slid up out of the floor, then another. A gas with a faint floral odor was being released.

Penrose drifted back in the chair.

The room was doing a smooth job of termination.

"Very efficient," said Penrose.